Nicholas Blincoe was born and grew up in North Manchester. He has worked in radio and newspapers and was once signed to Factory Records. He now lives in London.

Praise for ***Acid Casuals***

'Britain has as many baddies as anyone, and it's about time someone started writing novels about them. For that alone, Nicholas Blincoe deserves everyone's encouragement.' *The Observer* (Book of the Week)

'**** Best debut crime novel of the year . . . Blackly comic and highly inventive.' *Daily Telegraph*

'Another member of the growing blood and guts Serpent's Tail posse of young mystery writers . . . Decidedly the new face of British crime, and not for the faint-hearted.' *Time Out*

'A top buzz, as they used to say.' *i-D*

'Written with a confidence and power rare in a first novel. Blincoe evokes the slimy areas of nocturnal Manchester with passion; the dialogue is sharp and mega-hip.' *The Times*

'The novel of the Black Grape album. That says it all.' *Raw* (Book of the Year)

'Above all, there is Blincoe's style, which is consistently punchy and occasionally lyrical. An assured, confident début. (Great cover too).' *Time Out Web site*

'Throw in a transsexual assassin, some serious clubbing, even more serious drugs and one or two gangsters, decamp it all to the darker side of Manchester at the beginning of the nineties and you have the recipe for a delirious contemporary thriller.' *Big Issue*

'Reveals parts of Manchester that its tourist board doesn't include in its advertising . . . weirdly fascinating.' *Sunday Telegraph*

ACID CASUALS

Nicholas Blincoe

Library of Congress Catalog Card Number: 95-69752

A full catalogue record for this book can be obtained from
the British Library on request

First published in 1995 by Serpent's Tail,
4 Blackstock Mews, London N4, and
180 Varick Street, 10th floor, New York, NY 10014

Reprinted 1997

Set in 10pt ITC Century Book by CentraCet Ltd, Cambridge
Printed in Great Britain by Cox & Wyman Ltd, Reading,
Berkshire

For Robert Blincoe

ONE

'Yeah, Boss. On my way.' Amjad slung the radio handset on to the dashboard where his uncle's voice faded into the slurp of the windscreen wipers and the hot breath of the Nissan's air blowers. The rain hadn't let up, not all day.

When Amjad took the call, he was two minutes from the WARP bar. As he swung off Great Ancoats Street, it was just fifty yards ahead of him. Now he could see it, he was hoping the kid skipping around out front wasn't his fare. Dancing in the rain like that.

Amjad's cab slushed to a stop at the kerbside. The doors to the bar opened and a woman stepped out. Tall in her heels, she had a scarf wrapped over her head. Dancing Boy held the cab door open for her and she slipped inside, on to the acrylic tiger furs that covered the back seat. The boy followed her.

Amjad said, 'Where to, Chief?'

It was the woman who answered. 'Palatine Court, please. You find it behind the cancer hospital.'

'On my way, love.' Amjad stabbed the button on his fare meter and pulled away.

Amjad looked at the woman in his rear view mirror. Neither the accent nor her looks were English. He could have guessed she was foreign, even before she opened her mouth. If she'd been English, she wouldn't have been much to look at. English girls went for natural looks – either that or they slapped the make-up on with a trowel. She wore a ton of make-up and there was nothing natural about it but she was no dog. If she had been English she wouldn't have known what to make of herself. Not with her long, bony nose and the deep crescent lines down both her cheeks, either side of that huge mouth. This woman had made herself into a cinema queen. Sitting on Amjad's tiger skins, wrapped up in a big black scarf and hung with jewellery, she could pass as a film star easy.

She might be famous, you never knew. Maybe on the TV, perhaps she was a newscaster. What she was doing here, snogging some dumb kid she'd picked up in a bar, Amjad didn't know.

'Excuse me. You don't mind me asking – where you from, love?' he asked, half-turning over his shoulder.

'America.'

She didn't sound American. Amjad was going to ask her about that, but she spoke first.

'Why you have those beads hanging from the mirror? For luck? They balance your kharma?'

Amjad laughed and flicked at the chain of beads dangling in the middle of his windscreen. They were supposed to keep him safe and so far they had worked fine. He never crashed. He'd only ever had a few twats crash into him. No one had ever tried to shoot him.

'Keep us all safe, love.'

'Safe,' said the boy. He had a strong town accent, hissing the 's' and coming down hard on the 'f', but it was forced. He probably came from somewhere outside Manchester originally. Now that he had started talking, it was like he wanted to be the centre of attention: 'We're all safe, I got enough good kharma for everyone.'

The boy was definitely white. Amjad wasn't sure about the woman. She probably wasn't black, though. She didn't look Pakistani – nor Indian, Bangladeshi, whatever. He turned to look at her again, but they were back snogging.

Amjad kept quiet until he saw a diversion up ahead.

'I'm going to have to go a different way.'

The woman and her boyfriend pulled apart and looked over towards the police line. The area around the coach station was cordoned off with blue and white tape, flapping violently in the rain.

The woman said, 'What happened?'

Amjad shrugged, it could be anything: IRA, football fans, a fight, maybe a raid on one of the gay pubs down there. The boy began telling her the story of a rentboy who had leapt off the carpark above the coach station a month ago. Amjad knew all about it, he'd heard it was an accident not a suicide: the kid had thought he could fly, off his head on acid.

The woman continued to look around, even when the diversion was long behind them. Amjad was waiting at the lights on Whitworth Street when she asked, 'What happened to Central Station?'

The boy pointed. 'That building, there? That's G-Mex, Greater Manchester Exhibition Centre . . .' He broke off. 'You know Manchester, then?'

She admitted that she did. Although she hadn't seen it in a long time.

'I can tell. G-Mex was built over ten years ago.'

When Amjad stopped the cab in a cul-de-sac behind Christie's Hospital, she paid the fare and tip. As Amjad pulled his Nissan round, he saw her fitting the keys to the apartment door. The lad was hopping from foot to foot, his head turned up to the rain. He was dancing again. Off his fucking head for sure.

Estela turned as she opened the apartment door. She watched the cab ploughing water from the gutter, watched Yen splashing through puddles. She could not believe now how wet Manchester could get. She whistled and Yen danced up to her like a sweet little doggy.

'First floor, darling,' she said. Yen bounced up the steps ahead of her.

As they reached the apartment door, Estela held on to the back of Yen's jeans to slow him down. She span him around and they began kissing. His mouth tasted sweet and furry from all the fizzy drinks that she had bought him. She might have mixed him a martini from her duty-free drinks collection, but he had already told her he didn't touch alcohol. It was a pity, the gin might have disinfected his mouth. It would definitely have taken the edge off his manic, drugged energy.

'Should I skin up?' asked Yen.

Estela nodded. A joint might begin to mellow him out. She stepped over the suitcases that remained unpacked on the floor of the apartment, and found her plastic carrier bag of duty-free. She picked her way over to the kitchenette, then took an age to find the glasses – they were where she would have kept the kitchen cleaners, if this had been her own place.

'Boss stereo,' Yen shouted from the other side of the room, slotting a tape into the mouth of the machine.

Estela said, 'It came with the flat, I don' use it yet.'

Yen began playing with the buttons on the amplifier while Estela made herself a drink. She looked in the fridge for the olives she remembered putting there. Yen rolled around the living room floor trying to find the plug sockets. The stereo buzzed into life as Estela spun an unripe olive into her glass. It was some kind of electronic synthesiser music, with no kind of rhythm track at all.

Later, standing swaying in her bedroom, Yen said that he was sorted. Ambient sounds, a bit of spliff and he was coming down nicely. Estela felt good, too. Her jet-lag was beginning to loosen. She could feel the pressure spots on the soles of her feet unbind, releasing quiet waves of energy into her spine while she lay on the bed. She was surprised to find Yen's tape so relaxing. It was a kind of dance music, but without a beat – just splashes of repetitive noise like the soundtrack to a lost disco. She wondered how it would sound set to a rhumba. Sitting up at the edge of the bed, she took hold of Yen's thighs and drew him half a pace closer to her face. As he stood above her, she tapped the ends of her fingers in a light Latin beat on his buttocks. His penis jiggled in front of her, the long foreskin making its tip into a cute pink snout. He seemed to be in a trance. He was waving his arms slowly in the air, as though he were a piece of seaweed on the ocean bed, or a young tree in the breeze – some kind of spacey shit like that.

Estela pulled a condom out of her hairband. She carefully tore open the foil and, with the teat between her teeth, used her mouth to unroll it over Yen's springy erection. She let him dance in front of her, moving his penis in and out of her mouth. His trancey cosmic style was not a complete act, Yen was a gentle boy.

Yen fell asleep almost immediately. Estela did not mind. She had picked him up because she hated to nurse jet-lag alone but she was already feeling a thousand times better. She felt that she could easily fall asleep. Yen was spread over two-thirds of the double bed, slim and white against the sheets. He was very pretty. It was probably for the best that they had skipped full sex, after she had fellated him. Estela was still almost a virgin. She had not yet decided how best to approach the question of penetration. Through the finer and the coarser moments of her sex change operations, as she waited for her Brazilian doctors to pronounce themselves satisfied, she played safe and she waited. She felt, very soon, she would become as comfortable with the sex act as she already was with her new body. Tonight, her pantyhose stayed wrapped to her new curves. The protective layers of her underwear saved her any awkwardness.

She rolled on to her stomach, flattening her breasts beneath her. It took a moment before she found a way to get comfortable in the space between Yen's outstretched arm and his body. She let her own arm drift across his stomach and fell asleep before it reached the end of its line.

TWO

Estela was woken by the sun through the blinds. The latitude was all wrong. The light felt weak and she felt cold. Her travelling clock said Two. She had to squint to read the flashing 'p.m.' sign. She remembered having company when she fell asleep. She was alone now. The only thing on her pillow was a black mascara rash. Beyond the headboard, a sluttish reflection stared at her with streaky panda-eyes. In God's name, why were there so many mirrors in this flat? It was horrendous. Having to look at herself everywhere she turned, after three connecting flights and eighteen hours in the air. No wonder, once she arrived, she had run straight out again. She needed to find something to help her unwind.

Estela tripped out to the hallway, ignoring the used condom as she stood on it. She could tidy up details later. What she wanted to do, her primo priority, was dial herself another ten centigrade on the hallway thermostat. Before she left Manchester, the chill would have sunk straight through to her bones, she knew it.

When she took this job, she was promised a condo with all the extras: at least, a pool, a gym. She might take a photo of the dishwater-grey puddles outside her apartment. Show her boss what kind of swimming pool his dollars bought. He had no idea, he probably believed Manchester was like Miami. Maybe a little foggier. Whoever told him the apartment had a gym, they were taking a risk. If he found out that there was nothing but a nautilus machine in a room the size of a closet, someone was going to have to explain the joke. They could end up back in Medellin, putting bombs under judges and bishops. Héctor Barranco Garza preferred slapstick to most kinds of comedy.

When she reached the living room, she knew Yen was gone for good. Her suitcases were still spread over the floor, only now they were open and her clothes were thrown across the carpet. Jesus and Maria, she would have to go through every case to work out what the little bastard had stolen. Her life was nothing but annoyances.

Stepping over a case, Estela made for the bathroom and its wall of mirrors. She felt that she would faint if she did not rehydrate her poor, problem combination skin soon. All the magazines warn that air travel is unforgiving on the complexion. If she could be basted in ice-cold Evian, she would pay for someone to turn her over every five minutes.

The telephone rang before she was out of the shower. She grabbed a towel and wrapped her hair up into a high, white towelling turban. There was a matching bathrobe hanging behind the door. She found the telephone beneath an upturned Macy's bag.

'Manchester office,' she said, playing at secretaries.

'Estela? How you doing?' The confident, Hispanicised English of her boss. 'I hope you relaxed, already. They got you a good condo. It gotta pool?'

'It's too cold for swimming, Héctor. It's not stopped raining since I landed.'

'No shit. And you probably jet-lagged to fuck, huh? I thought you never going to get to the phone.'

'I'm a little slow this morning, Héctor. I took something to help me sleep last night. But once I get to work, I'll be nursing my jet-lag by the side of your pool inside two days.'

'I would love to see you by the pool, baby. I send the boys out for a tube of bathing milk and spread it over you with my tongue.'

Garza was in a good mood, playing it up in English. But he never let business details drift away in small talk.

'You got the package?'

Estela guessed so.

'What d'you mean, you not looked? Santa Maria, Estela, get on the fucking page. It's only a satellite connection, let me hang on the fucking phone while you go look. Don' worry, I got better things I gotta do today.'

Estela dropped the handset to the floor and started for the bedroom. Garza's voice continued to spill out of the earpiece and on to the carpet. She ran back for the receiver: 'Sorry, Héctor?'

'I said, you got conference? Put the phone on conference. You think I'm some loco schizz-nutzoid, I wanna talk to myself.'

Estela prodded the loudspeaker button at the front of the telephone. Garza's voice followed her as she picked her way back to the spare bedroom. He shouted that she knew the procedure. What was her problem? She want to go see one of her fancy five-star pussy doctors – she wanna plead PMT, the fucking menopause or what? Estela knew the procedure, it was just that she wasn't feeling altogether one hundred per cent. Garza had insisted she handle this job personally. She had never wanted to fly to England but Garza said this kind of business could not be trusted to a franchisee. It had to be done in-house.

'Get with it, Estela. A job like this, I do it before breakfast. I do it between waking and walking to the fucking john, give my woody time to slack off. I hear you talk about England. I figure you know your way around, at leas' how to act cool. Or what counts as cool, around Anglo-Protestant assholes.'

Estela recalled the whole conversation now. Garza did not think that Manchester was Miami in a fog. He thought the whole of England was like Boston, which he had visited once. In town just three hours, he had upended the *maître d'* of the hotel restaurant in a bouillabaisse. Outraged, he could not believe the way the man had acted. If anyone thought that kind of behaviour was going to be tolerated – well, Héctor Barranco Garza pitied the whole fucking town. Estela could see him now, arms frozen in a shrug: I mean, the fuck is this. He had been looking forward to the trip. He imagined that everyone would look like Cary Grant or Grace Kelly, or perhaps Charles Laughton. He thought he would get to see some classy interpersonal skills in effect. Estela had tried to imagine Cary Grant with Charles Laughton, maybe a Grace Kelly sandwich trick. Visited by a full premonition, warning the Boston trip would end badly, Estela took a swerve by pleading business in Miami.

She walked into the smaller bedroom, expecting to find an attaché case in the closet. She did not expect to see it on the nautilus machine, wide open. She felt her knees go weak, looking at it lying there.

Yen had been through the case. There was no doubt, he had not tried to cover his thieving tracks. Where there should have been a Beretta, there were only a few scattered papers. Otherwise, the case was empty.

Garza's voice didn't give her the time she needed to think. She shouted that she had it; yes, yes. Garza could not have heard her, he was bellowing What? What? She scrambled the case and the papers together and hugged it closed as she ran back to the living room.

'I got it, Héctor.'

'Yeah? You got the folder?'

The photographs were no longer in the manila envelope. They were loose and turned frontwards, backwards, every way but the right way. She shuffled them around and looked down at the face of the man she was supposed to kill. Whoever put the package together had helpfully typed the name on each photograph, along with an arrow pointing to Mr John Burgess's head. A marked man, the arrows pointing him out in a crowd and indicating the trajectory of a bullet. They could have left the graphics alone; Estela already knew his name.

She had to seem calm, there was no need to panic. She believed in fate, in the stars and their psycho-magnetic influence. She could play this, once she had seen the way the astral forces were spinning.

'Estela?'

'One second, Héctor, honey. These high-heels aren' made for running after men.'

'Let them run to you, huh? You do it your way, baby. Let him come over, you knock him back.'

Estela looked at the photographs again. Every last one showed the owner of the bar where she had cruised Yen the night before. John Burgess had placed his own picture high on the wall where he could smile beatifically down on his punters. She knew him. Worse, Yen knew him.

She needed to think this through. Yen had looked at the photographs. No doubt. But would he put it all together? Gun plus photo equals one dead man; bang, bang, bang. Estela rechecked the contents of the case. Apart from the Beretta, nothing seemed to be missing. Yen might have taken a photograph, she could not tell, but he probably had not.

'No problems?'

'Fine, Héctor. Tell me, what does our associate do?'

'Fuck, Estela. This is no secret code line, we speaking

in the open-fucking-air. You heard of spy satellites. He's a money man, is all.'

'He has some financial tools? He's prepared to offer his services to a higher bidder?'

'Tha' kind of shit, yeah. He wants to break an exclusive care contract previously negotiated with us. He go to auction, he give our competitors the same advantage in the European market we got. We wanna keep it proprietal. Okay?'

'Okay, Héctor. I'll see you soon. One, two days.'

'Okay, baby. You know I wan' you back by the pool. Until then, all the saints preserve you.'

She switched off the phone line and stared back into the case. All that was left inside was a plastic container with the raised logo Fempax, a tampon manufacturer. Her bullets were inside. As long as no stray bullet had been racked into the chamber, the Beretta was harmless. Estela did not know why Yen had avoided the tampon box. Maybe he was squeamish. If he was too stupid to check it out, that was in his favour.

Estela hoped that Yen was stupid. Really, really stupid. She would have to hunt him down, of course. The second she had put on her face, perhaps straightened the flat. It looked as though she might be in Manchester for a little longer than she had anticipated. She might as well make herself comfortable.

Yen sat on the office desk, swinging his legs and looking at the bottle of pills he had taken from his pocket. Theresa could clearly see the whitish capsules crowded on the inside of the brown glass, but it was obvious Yen did not know what they were. He was staring at the labelless bottle, his face blanker than usual.

The offices lay beneath the club in the old cellars with their curved bricked ceilings, a reminder that the Gravity had been a warehouse, before it was renovated and remodelled. Theresa and Yen sat on one side of the office, opposite the bank of TVs ranked along the facing wall, waiting for the show to start. It was Junk who invited them downstairs. He had asked if they wanted to view his latest video. Now he was crouched on the floor, stabbing at the VCR machine, his one good eye and his one glass eye fixed to the flashing green arrow. Junk had worked at the club since it opened and had access to the offices. It made Theresa nervous, trespassing downstairs. It didn't bother Yen, he was only worried about his pills.

Yen held the bottle up. 'What do you think they are?'

Junk turned away from the machine, he had no idea. 'What do I know? Why don't you ask the woman who gave them you?'

Yen said, 'Maybe. I don't know if I'm seeing her again.'

'Who was she?'

'I don't remember. She wasn't from round here.' Yen mimed a flamenco, clicking castanets. 'Hispaniola or something. You know. Riva, Riva, El Mariachi.'

Yen emptied a clutch of the pills on to his hand and sniffed at them. Talking aloud, he said the woman wasn't freaked by drugs. If she was Latino, maybe the pills were cocaine: straight outta Colombia and only moulded to look like standard pharmaceuticals. Although there could only be twenty-five grammes in total: the bottle held fifty pills.

'Or they could be barbiturates. Valium or, you know, some equivalent.'

Theresa let him talk, watching him gape at the pills through his floppy fringe. She could guess what had happened. Once he was inside the woman's flat, he would wait until she was asleep and run through her medicine cabinet. Theresa was the same as age as Yen but it was only after meeting him that she began to feel especially mature. He was dreaming if he thought they were cocaine. If he honestly thought they were valium, let him experiment.

'Well, what are they?'

Theresa shrugged. She knew Yen would try a couple. Even a handful, just as he had with those anti-psychotic pills last year. He pronounced them Halaperadol and had snapped back more than a dozen. An hour and a half later, Yen's jaw had gone into a spasm, his teeth virtually welded together. His mouth took on a horrendous Jack Nicholson grin that had grown more and more painful through the night. The doctor described the side-effect as *sardonicus rictus*, although it was another forty-eight hours before Yen admitted himself to hospital. Until then, he had rolled a comic book into a tube and forced it between his teeth. It did nothing to stop the upper teeth from grinding against the lower ones. The comic ended up with a mouth-size chunk bitten out of its centre.

Theresa would have reminded Yen of that time but even he could not have forgotten. The whole medical staff at the hospital, doctors and nurses, came out to look at the idiot who had swallowed a case-load of Halaperadol. Theresa kept Yen company but made him tell the doctors himself what was wrong. It wasn't that she minded too much being associated with a moron. She had thought it would be funny, watching him trying to talk like a mad ventriloquist, pronouncing the name of the drug through clenched teeth. It was funny. Especially when the first injection of antidote only partially worked and his tongue began to loll uncontrollably out from his painful smile. But she wasn't in a hurry to go through it again.

Yen put the bottle away and started work on a joint. It was neatly rolled and trimmed inside a few seconds but it was Theresa who had to find an ashtray.

Junk's tape had spooled to its beginning. He pressed Play and a selection of cartoons flashed on screen. They seemed to be elongated, as though they had been stretched for cinescope. Bugs Bunny was short and fat and moved with a pensive waddle. Theresa didn't know how Junk had made him do that.

Junk stood up and stretched, looking over at Yen. 'Careful where you leave the roach. I don't want Burgess to know I'm using his office during the day.

Back in her bathroom, Estela found her supply of Chicadol was missing. She could weep. They were the best hormone pills she'd ever found. They gave her the best shape she'd ever seen.

THREE

Down to the Mancunian Way, through the underpass with its strange cobbled hillocks – some kind of urban design feature – and up into Hulme. Junk walked everywhere. He kept his head down as he took his long stepping strides, his hands in the pockets of his snorkel jacket and his waterproof satchel dangling at his back. To the right, just out of sight, was his own flat. Beyond were the remains of the Crescents, the huge blocks that, uninhabitable or squatted, had lately been demolished. On the left, slung over Princess Park Way, was the narrow footbridge where gangs would wait at night to tax crossing pedestrians. On the far side was Junk's lock-up, a garage he had rented from a small ad in a free paper. He only visited his lock-up once a week and only ever in the early morning when no one was around to see him. He found that most people liked to get to bed by five or six a.m.

Junk reached shelter at Moss Side Shopping Centre. Across Hulme and Moss Side, the rain was coming down in heavy sheets like the lead lining around a casket. He put his hand to the base of his pony tail and squeezed down until the water ran off the end. He would have put his hood up, but he knew he looked like a fool when he did that. He checked the fastener on his satchel. The ounce of amphetamine sulphate, twenty-five grammes, was safe and dry; snapped shut, as an extra precaution, inside a video case labelled *Straw Dogs*. That was why Junk had visited his lock-up that morning: to fetch the speed and measure it out with his plastic jug. There had looked to be a couple of kilos left in the fridge, hidden at the back of the garage under a tarpaulin. It was almost all gone. Was that good or bad? Fuck knows.

He had always thought that he might be tempted, but had never once touched as much as a speck of his secret speed stash. It would be twelve years now, about that, since he had last taken amphetamines. Although he still hadn't put the weight back on again.

Junk trotted past the few working shops and the empty stores between them. He re-entered the rain on Moss Lane East. The gym where he was meeting his gangsta connection was directly to his right. He always felt stupid as he walked inside. It wasn't just that he was white, or even that he was so thin, but somehow he felt he was an insult to the boys who trained there. They worked at their repetitions, counting under their breath as they lifted, jerked, pulled or punched. Junk grew self-conscious of his own irregular rhythms, his skittery habits that grew out of an excessively nervous system.

Junk tried to make himself inconspicuous as he sat down on a bench, watching a sparring session and waiting for the Taz-Man and his posse to show.

The two boys in the ring were really slamming into each other. An old man with a strong Jamaican accent, pork-pie hat and a Fila sweatsuit was jumping around in excitement, shouting instructions through the ropes. Neither of the two boys could be listening. How could they? They were hammering away, they didn't have time to listen. Junk stared ahead until he went blank.

It was strange, last night in the WARP, believing that he recognised Yen's woman. A thing like that could come out of nowhere, a retinal snapshot that you'd see once and be incapable of erasing; extra proof that your mind was never quite your own. She had not seen him, even when she brushed past him on her way to the cab. Another snapshot, the tiger skin seatcovers at the back of the old Nissan. Junk had watched through the open door, as Yen and the Hispanic woman got inside. And then another flash as the driver turned his head to check the passing traffic and Junk caught sight of the tiger skin headrest above the driver's seat. Vibrant orange, overprinted black; like the robe draped over the blue corner post ahead of him. No, not quite like that. The boxer's robe was silk, napless and smooth. The taxi seats were acrylic fur.

The Taz-Man's voice came from somewhere off to Junk's blind side, 'The Junkmeister. How're you doing, you all right or what?'

Junk jerked round. 'Yeah, I'm all right, Taz.'

The Taz-Man stood at the entrance to the changing room. He filled the bottom half of the doorway; other members of the ConCho Heavy were visible above his head. Junk stood and walked over when he was beckoned.

The Taz-Man had taken a seat on the double bench at the centre of the changing rooms. Three members of his posse gathered around him. Towards the far wall, there was a boy wrapped in a towel, steam coming off his wet shoulders as he looked through his locker. The Taz-Man looked over to his lieutenant. 'Tell him to do one.' He nodded at the boy. A moment later, the boy was shivering in the main room of the gym, skipping up and down in just a towel. Trying not to catch a chill.

The Taz-Man said, 'Look at him. Fucking Batty Boy, couldn't fight Chewie's sister.'

The Taz-Man's lieutenant was saying, 'No, couldn't fight my baby sister.'

'I don't know why he shows round here.'

'Fucking Batty Boy.'

A locker to the Taz-Man's left had the 'C' sign of the

ConCho Heavy sprayed on the door. The Taz-Man rapped it. 'Subtle eh? Open it up, Chewie.'

Chewie took a key to the heavy duty padlock. The guns inside hung from hooks by their shoulder straps. There were loose magazines and assorted handguns piled at the bottom of the locker.

'Sweet, eh? Fucking bootcamp, this. Chewie's the quartermaster. You've come in the middle of us planning a mission.'

Junk said, 'I've come at the time I always come.'

'It's sweet. Just letting you know what kind of motherfuckers we turning into. Every month, you come down and we're a little more fucked up than the last time. Soon we going to be as crazy as you.'

Junk looked back in the locker. The Taz-Man was right about one thing: every month they were more fucked up.

'Now you seen it, we'll go and do the dirty deal. What you got for me this month?'

FOUR

A conversation in the WARP.

'I don't understand these video games. My little brother, right, he's hooked up to his Megadrive twelve hours a day. I've got to drag him off by his fucking ears otherwise I can't watch the telly. And the thing is, right, television is something you watch but a video game is something that watches you. You know what I mean?'

'No.'

The redhead was a conspiracy theorist. He worked away at his theme while he sucked at the quarter of lemon sticking out of the top of his beer bottle. The other one, the dark haired boy, had a less manic style. He leant well back in his chair, keeping the redhead in perspective through lazy blue eyes. The redhead began to elaborate, picking lemon pips out of his teeth as he talked.

'Like video games are a trip, right. So they're addictive. And they're also a machine. So my brother's having his reality reconfigured according to machine code, right.'

'You sound like the kind of freak who goes on Donahoe. Now you're saying video games are addictive. Last week you were telling me you didn't even believe drugs are addictive.'

'They're not. It's just the power of suggestion, right, if you believe they're addictive, then you'll get addicted.' The redhead paused. 'Anyway, all I know, since my brother got into video games, my mum's stopped worrying about where I am, the state I'm in or the time I get back – she's more scared he'll catch epilepsy from playing Sonic the Hedgehog.'

The dark boy seemed to wake up, shaking his beer bottle like a maraca as he recalled the program: 'Sonic, he's the blue hedgehog, yeah? . . . I've seen that. I can't believe it's so fast. I tell you, those video games only appeal to kids because they're too young to drive down motorways on acid.'

The redhead was nodding vigorously. The dark boy had a smile around his eyes, leaning back again, watching how his friend reacted. Estela noticed how slender his fingers looked, holding the neck of a beer bottle.

The WARP was a converted furniture shop, around three times as deep as it was broad. The granite bartop to her left ran along the whole length of the whole building. The style of the bar was what they termed post-industrial, meaning that it had yards of bare masonite and the tabletops were panes of reinforced wire glass. The lighting was great. When Estela cruised through the previous night, she had seen Yen directly. She'd thought mmmmmm, that would smooth the kinks out of twenty hours of airflight. That's why she had headed back to the WARP this evening. As soon as she found him, he had better hope there was a place among the angels for light-fingered space cadets.

Tonight, at a little after five o'clock, the bar had not begun to fill. Estela saw the redhead conspiracist and recognised him as a friend of Yen's. The darker boy was speaking as she strolled up.

'You've got hair round your lips, and now you're talking like a cunt.'

Estela looked over at the redhead as she sat down. He had a goatie beard, too pale to see unless you were close. The dark one blushed as Estela sat, a boy who preferred not to say 'cunt' in front of a woman. Estela smiled and said hello.

'I believe I remember you both from las' night. I was with a frien' of yours called Yen. Today . . .' Estela leant closer, the two boys did the same. '. . . I found he left a little bag in my apartment and it was full of marijuana. Now, I don' know what to do. I was thinking, shall I smoke it, shall I return it? Or shall I share it out?'

Estela dropped her packet on to the table top. A small block of resin wrapped inside the kind of plastic envelope banks use to separate and weigh five pounds' worth of silver. It had taken her all of five minutes to buy the dope, from leaving her apartment to closing the deal. The cab driver had been absurdly helpful – taking her to the door of a Moss Side pub and even offering to score for her while she waited in the cab. She had laughed, really he didn't have to be so protective. She was a modern woman.

'Share, I reckon.' The dark boy smiled, and put his hand over the envelope. Estela smiled back.

'But not here,' he said. 'The management's beginning to get edgy about smoking.'

'Then we share it some other time. It's only fair. It's not as though Yen was so wonderful last night I feel eternally grateful to him.' She stretched out her hand. 'My name is Estela.'

The redhead was Tom, the one with the beautiful hands was called Cozy. Of the two, it was Cozy who remembered her, not Tom. He had seen her last night, as she talked to Yen in the window alcove. Estela told him he should have come over, there was no reason to be shy.

She sat with them for the few hours it took the WARP to fill. Different kids, aged from seventeen to around twenty-two, drifted by. Some would join them, some would just touch hands, laughing over something and ending by saying, 'Safe, see you later.' Yen never arrived but when she mentioned him again, Tom said he would be along. Either that or he'd be at the Gravity. It was a while before Estela understood that the Gravity was a night-club at the far end of town. Cozy and Tom's friends had started to talk about a girl named Theresa.

'She's sound.'

'She's a bit mad.'

She's got a mad touch, but she's sound.

Estela heard that Theresa helped put on video shows at the Gravity. There was an argument about whether Yen was seeing her, or whether he just hung out with her so he could meet the DJs. Cozy said, 'Yeah, that was it, Yen's just a total DJ-groupie'. He would offer to roll their spliffs or carry their record cases, 'then rip them off'. Estela agreed it sounded like Yen, from the little she knew of him.

Cozy told Estela they'd be moving along to the Gravity after, she should come along. Estela was happy to stick around their crowd. She recognised a few of Tom and Cozy's friends from the previous night. She found them likeable, friendly. The ones who were stupid made her laugh, the ones who were not stupid made her laugh as well.

Everyone took an interest in her. She blushed, but could easily stand the glare. They asked where she was from, what she did. When she told them she was a cleaner, looking after a couple of old businessmen out in Florida, they laughed. She didn't look like a cleaner, wearing a Betty Jackson suit, its straightness relieved by chunky touches of gold. Estela had learnt not to feel out of place. Tonight she felt relaxed. Her various problems, the disarray that jet-lag, alcohol and unhinged libido had injected into her first night in England, all that could be tidied up.

When she offered to buy a new round of drinks about half the table asked for health drinks. Estela stuck to martinis, gin and French. At the bar, just as she was being served, she turned to find Cozy hovering behind her. He said he could help her carry the drinks.

'Thank you. You're sweet.'

The photograph of John Burgess sneered down at Estela's mixed order: ginseng juices and Lucozades, gin vermouth and two bottles of Mexican beer. As she paid, Estela waved her credit card towards the picture, 'Who's he?'

'The boss.'

Lit from beneath and set within a twelve-by-eight-inch black frame, the photograph had a solemn, in memoriam, appeal. With his strained smile, Burgess already looked as though he had been glazed by a mortician. Estela asked Cozy again: 'Who?'

'John Burgess. This is his bar, and the Gravity is his club. He's a big Manchester businessman, a one-man Mecca. Into all kinds of stuff. You see him here, sometimes.'

Not today; Estela had been scanning the bar all evening. She had not seen Burgess. She had seen young men in clothes that looked as if they'd been slept in, clutching mobile phones. Evidence of low-level drug dealing. And she remembered what Cozy had told her about dope.

'I thought, the management, they don' care for drugs.'

Cozy said, 'They're not on a crusade. But Burgess has to renew his licences every year and for the past two the police and the council have given him jip. He has to play safe. The bouncers throw out anyone caught dealing. Burgess has security cameras over at the Grav.'

Cozy shrugged. It really wasn't a problem.

'If you want to do a trip or an E, you buy one at any of the pubs round there. Once you're inside the club, you drop it, you're sorted. No one's going to search two thousand people to see who's carrying a tab inside their sock. You've just got to be careful. If you're not going to give the bouncers grief, they're not going to worry about what you do. They just don't want a repeat of that thing from a couple of years back.'

Estela didn't know what happened two years ago. Cozy told her it was all over the papers.

'Not the *Miami Herald*.'

Cozy nodded, he guessed not. 'A girl died in the Gravity. She had an allergic reaction to Ecstasy. A friend's sister works down the hospital and saw the autopsy report. The girl died of massive internal haemorrhaging.' Cozy shuddered. 'Now, if anyone passes out from the heat or drink, anything, the bouncers go mental. They're scared they've got another death on their hands.'

Estela took another look at John Burgess's picture before signalling Cozy to carry the tray. 'So Burgess likes to keep a drug-free image?'

Cozy explained as he followed Estela back to their table: 'He has to, or he loses his licence. Especially after all the Gunchester stuff in the papers. You haven't heard of that either . . . No? . . . The gangs on Moss Side have been shooting each other. There's other gangs from Salford and Cheetham Hill who've got guns as well. A year back, a lad rushed the Gravity with a shotgun. No one knows if it was loaded. He was just off his head. He ran in the club waving the gun, then he just did one. The police didn't catch him. No one identified him. Just some dickhead from Salford. It's not as if it was an Uzi or anything, it was just an old shotgun.'

Estela made room for Cozy as she took her seat. 'Shotguns work as well as anything.'

Cozy looked at her, his sweet blue eyes a little round now. Estela smiled sweetly.

Cozy smiled back. 'Yeah. It must seem tame after Miami. With *Scarface* and that.

Estela had seen the film. Not all the way through. She had met people who watched nothing else and could recite whole scenes, even if they couldn't spell alpacino.

'Here is nicer than Miami. Apart from the weather. Perhaps I should ask for a brandy and port, the next time.

She and Cozy left for the Gravity by taxi; Tom came along as well. Their friends had walked and both Tom and Cozy would have too, normally. It was Estela who insisted on the taxi; she did not want to wander out in the rain. The cab looped around Piccadilly Gardens. Estela watched the girls in bare legs huddle close to the walls, trying to keep their hair from getting wet. The men stood in two-tone shirts, grouped in packs, blinking as their hair gel dissolved and ran into their eyes. She wondered if the Gravity was one of those clubs that made people queue outside. Cozy told her not to worry.

'The queue goes right round the block, but I'm on the guest list so we'll get straight in.'

Tom turned around in the front passenger seat. He said, 'We're fucking stars. We don't wait in line.'

'It's not that.' Cozy had an attractive way of blushing. Normally, it wouldn't have worked on her. Estela felt she must be getting sentimental for England. He explained, 'Burgess gives a free pass to anyone who works for him. That's why we get in the Grav for free.'

He hadn't mentioned that he worked for Burgess.

'We both work in his travel agents, Med-Liberty on Corporation Street. It's dead easy. And with the perks . . . well, there's worse places to work.'

Tom said, 'A lot fucking worse. I do fuck all, me.'

Estela could not imagine anyone employing a moron

like Tom, but she was getting bitter. It was easier to shed your skin than lose Tom. She should ask more questions about the travel agency, she really should. Before she could formulate one, Cozy said that Yen worked there too.

Estela felt herself sag; a second earlier she been pertly buoyant. She had pretty much dismissed the news that Yen spent all of his time in either the WARP or the Gravity, although they were both owned by Burgess. Now she was told that he spent his days working for the man as well. 'Yen's very friendly with Burgess.'

Cozy looked at her, what did she mean by 'friendly'? 'Because he hangs out at the Gravity? He's a bit friendly with some of Burgess's people, I suppose. He spends a lot of time with Junk.'

'Who's Junk?'

'He puts together the videos they show at the Gravity. Yen met him through Theresa, who's Junk's assistant. But you'll have seen Junk last night, he was in the bar when you came in. Tall and skinny, pock-marked. He's only got one eye.'

Estela hadn't seen Junk. Not at all. While she flounced around, playing the tart and flirting with every spaced-out teen geek she met, this job was spinning wildly out of control. She had to formulate a strategy before she became utterly disorientated. Everything about the Burgess job was disorientating her. Even Manchester no longer looked the same.

FIVE

Junk had to take the corner chair. Burgess had the best seat but it was his office. When Junk returned, he had found Burgess just as he was now. Swivelling in his chair, keeping the whole of the club under surveillance. Stacked on their shelf at the far end of the room, the six TV sets showed different views of every corner of the Gravity. Burgess turned away from the one he'd been watching – an overhead shot of the main door.

'What do you think he's doing?' Burgess asked.

Junk leant over to the TV; the figure just seemed to be scratching himself.

Burgess said, 'He's been scratching himself like that for ten minutes. What do you think is wrong with him?'

'I don't know. Lice. A rash. How should I know?' Junk didn't even know why he was being asked.

'Well do you think we should tape it, sit him down there, play it back to him and ask him what his problem is?'

'Why?'

'He's supposed to be security. If he can't keep his fucking dick clean, what good is he?'

Junk kept quiet. He didn't see the link between strict personal hygiene and working as a bouncer. But then, he'd never thought about it before. If Burgess believed the connection was significant, presumably he had his reasons. Burgess had a head for that stuff and Junk didn't necessarily follow the line of thought. Half the time, he had enough trouble following his own line of thought.

'Would you sack him?' asked Burgess.

'No, I wouldn't sack him,' said Junk. 'Why are you asking me?'

'It's an aptitude test. I'm seeing whether intense exposure to my management techniques has given you an insight into the clubs and leisure industry.'

'It hasn't,' said Junk.

He'd known Burgess for nearly twenty years. He had thought, once, that he knew how to run a club. Hire a DJ, put a bouncer on the door, scoop the notes out of the till at three a.m. and pay off everyone who required it. You would walk off with a roll in your pocket, easy, and out into the night. Burgess had told him those days were long gone. Junk reckoned so, too. He was on the pay roll, now. When he picked up his wages, he took out a slip and read that his tax and national insurance contributions had been deducted. It seemed sacrilegious, working nights in a club and paying national insurance like anyone who clocked on and off for a living. Even the DJs were businesslike. They described themselves as freelancers and hired accountants to negotiate their tax schedules.

Junk pulled his satchel around on to his knee. The video cassettes stacked inside were labelled with sticky freezer labels. Junk reached to the bottom of the bag, found the couple of wraps of cocaine he had made up at home and put them on Burgess's desk. Burgess looked over at them. He already had a wad of notes in his hand. Peeling off a few twenties, he handed them over his shoulder. 'Eighty quid, Junk.'

That was right. And another eighty tomorrow when the cocaine was gone and Burgess needed more. Junk took the notes and slipped them into the front of his satchel.

Burgess said, 'What else have you got in there?'

Junk picked out one of his videos: 'Some Manga flicks that a friend brought back from Japan, snatches of a Czech surrealist short I taped off the BBC and a Gerard Damiano fest'.' Junk was pretty pleased with the tape he'd edited together for tonight.

Almost ten years ago, Burgess had told Junk he was opening a new club and had a great idea. He was going to have a VJ as well as a DJ, playing videos which would be projected on to screens above the dance floor. Burgess had read about VJs working the clubs of New York and Tokyo. At the time, Junk was pirating video porn for spare change. Burgess hired Junk when he heard about the videoing mixing desk that Junk had built in his flat.

Thanks to Burgess, Junk had become almost famous. Music papers came to interview him. TV producers would buy his tapes and even offer him work. They were a little nonplussed when they found out he was blind in one eye as a result of injecting amphetamine sulphate directly into his eyeball. But it made a good story. Junk never did move over into TV – what would he be doing anyway, editing together promos for sports programmes, step aerobics from Venice Beach or something? He was happier in the club, with his own VJ booth and editing suite.

Burgess had got excited about Junk's work immediately. He had got into the habit of borrowing Junk's latest tapes. Burgess said, 'Well I don't watch telly, it's too slow: I need something with a touch more intensity.'

Anyone who saw Burgess, they'd think: late-forties, successful. They might even admire his suit. But they would never see his house. It wasn't only that it was so stark, rather than comfortably domestic. It was the TV sets. Burgess really did play Junk's tapes all the time: snatches of skate videos, monster truck marathons, porno movies, kung fu and Chinese ghost films, Russian cartoons – all cut together into a schizophrenic orgy. It was the only thing that Burgess had in common with Junk. That, and not sleeping.

John Burgess was ten years older than Junk and looked like a florid version of Steve Martin, but without the kind of personality that you'd want to let grow on you. It seemed to Junk that he'd known the man all his life. That was his luck. Making the videos was the compensation for the nastier shit he put up with.

Burgess said, 'See that, the bastard did it again. He's had his hands on his cock all evening. What's going to happen when the punters roll up? He'll be so busy playing with himself the Ponderosa Liberation Army could walk past launching anti-tank rockets and he'd wave them through. That's why I had the metal detectors installed.'

Junk screwed up his good eye, he found watching the security cameras a little slow. They improved later in the evening, when the club was full. But only if you could flick between all the cameras very quickly, which was impossible. Each camera had its own VCR and monitor. Junk twitched his head back and forth, blinking at the same time. It was an unsatisfactory solution, it hurt his neck and so he stopped. The club was beginning to fill. The cavernous dance floor was empty but, looking at the monitors for the cafeteria and two of the bars, he could see the seats in the quieter corners of the club were already taken – mostly by regulars, friends, people who could skip the queue and walk right past security with a nod and a scratch. He saw Yen and Theresa, sat in the upstairs bar. But the paying punters would take an hour or more to get inside.

Sitting swivelling on his high bar stool, Yen was telling Theresa that the pills had had no effect – they were probably Ibuprofen tablets that his Latino lover had bought to relieve her period pains.

'How many did you take?' asked Theresa.

'I don't know,' said Yen. 'Enough.'

He sucked at the neck of his Lucozade bottle. Theresa watched him. He hadn't a clue, sitting on his bar stool, swinging his legs. He looked about four years old. The clothes he wore, a sweatshirt down to his knees and loose skate pants, made him look like a toddler. He pulled the bottle away from his mouth and grinned at her. Even his teeth looked babyish; milky white, small and evenly separated.

He brushed his hair out of his eyes. 'Let's have a smoke. We can sit in Junk's video room, he won't mind.'

Theresa nodded, okay. She knew Junk wouldn't mind, although all the staff at the Gravity had been warned about smoking dope on the premises. Burgess had said that he was covering for no one, no way. Now that he had installed video cameras, he was almost wildly enthusiastic about letting the police view playbacks of the tapes he made. The only safe, camera-free rooms were in the club's cellars, among the dressing rooms and offices, or above the dance floor in the DJ booth and Junk's room. Yen had already tried skinning-up in the DJ booth but, as usual, he had been kicked out. Last year, a world-famous DJ from Detroit accused Yen of lifting records behind his back and now none of the DJs trusted him. Theresa thought it was likely that Yen was guilty, although she had never seen him do it.

Of everyone who worked at the Gravity, about the only person who still got on with Yen was Junk. Well, most of the girls and some of the gays behind the bar liked him but even they were careful where they left their bags when he was around. But Junk was weirdly tolerant of Yen. He was weirdly tolerant of just about anything, but especially of Yen. Theresa had thought that maybe it was because Yen was her friend, and so Junk let him hang around for her sake. She now thought that Junk just liked having Yen around, someone who appeared even more stupid than him. Caught between the two of them, Theresa felt like the side order on a moron sandwich. Although Junk wasn't stupid exactly, just a little fried.

'Junk's room will be open, won't it?' asked Yen.

'It doesn't matter, I've got the key,' said Theresa.

'Nice one, Tréz!'

Yen was already bouncing off along the balcony towards Junk's booth. Theresa slid off her bar stool and followed him. The cocktail bar opened on to a wide gantry that overlooked the dance floor. At the far end were three booths, one for the lighting boys, one for the DJ and then Junk's private room. Yen was halfway across the gantry now, hanging over the balustrade and waving at someone over the other side of the club. Theresa looked over the edge, into the gaping space below. The Gravity was about a quarter full. It would take another hour, then it would be heaving.

'Hey, come on, Tréz.' Yen was pulling at Theresa's sleeve.

He almost dragged her to the VJ booth. Theresa couldn't help laughing at him, saying to him: You dick, Yen.

'Yeah, yeah, yeah, come on, let's toke. You know it makes sense.'

Jumping up and down on the spot, Theresa opened the door and he rushed through.

Inside Junk's video cabin, Theresa ran her finger over the tapes, labelled and racked on shelves. She didn't know how Junk had built his collection, where he found the tapes or how he afforded them. The collection filled the shelves on three walls of the cabin. The only free space held Junk's mixing desk and, above it, a huge window that opened out to the club below. Junk would sit up here, watching his tapes run on the screens above the dance floor. Calling him a VJ made it sound as though he mixed and edited the tapes on the spot. In fact, he did that during the day. At night he just sat back and enjoyed them. Junk was a master. Theresa studied video at college but she had learnt more from him than from her tutors. His mixing desk was certainly better than anything at college, even if its layout was a little counter-intuitive, at least from her point of view.

Yen sat in Junk's control seat, playing at Mission Control, running his hands over the buttons and looking out of the window.

'Mach speed, baby, we're going in . . . No, skipper, I can't hold it. There's no juice in the tanks and we took some flak in the fin . . . We few, we band of brothers. Ah ha, cry havoc and unleash the dogs of war.'

With the last roll of the 'r' of war, Yen shot out his tongue, licked down the edge of his double-width Rizla paper and sealed the joint. Theresa could never believe how quickly Yen did that; she hadn't even seen him begin to roll it. No one could skin up faster than Yen. He should try card tricks, sleight of hand, something. I mean, you couldn't say he was completely untalented.

'Let's fire it up.'

Yen was holding the joint in one hand, a nickel-plated pistol in the other.

SIX

Burgess cut a line of cocaine on the desktop: 'Do you want a share of this?'

Junk shook his head. These Saturday evening chats were beginning to grind him down. He disliked having to sit back in this windowless basement office and listen to Burgess when he could be in his cabin in the sky, his own video nirvana. Burgess had only initiated these Saturday sessions because he relied on Junk for his dripfeed of cocaine. Burgess was careful never to hold so much as a gramme, and he didn't want to know where it came from.

'You sure I can't tempt you?' said Burgess again, straightening two lines with the edge of his credit card.

'I'm sure. I've decided I'm too low-rent for cocaine,' said Junk, wondering if he had listened to Burgess for long enough. Could he leave?

'Look at them.' Burgess was pointing at the video monitor; the camera gave an aerial shot of the club entrance. 'What do they think they look like?'

The queue outside the club was shuffling forward. What they looked like was: a gang of renegade athletes fallen seriously foul of the doping laws, or a pack of new age travellers who'd caught a good deal on shop-soiled XXL sportswear. Junk switched his gaze from the monitor back to Burgess and watched him trace down the white line of cocaine with a rolled note. Who first thought of doing that, noseing down into a powdery dust? Was Burgess replaying a prehistoric ritual, updating it with large denomination bank notes, but basically re-enacting an original part of native South American folklore? Hunched over his desk with a fifty in his nostril, navigating a channel straight from his nasal membranes to his brain, was Burgess putting roots down into an ancient civilisation, connecting himself to the shamans and ghosts of Amazonia? If it was some kind of Aztec or Inca custom, it might work better if the stuff was blasted into your nose through a blow pipe. Junk thought that if he got hold of the pipe, he could take the top clean off Burgess's head. He watched the tears stream out of Burgess's two eyes, watched him wipe the tip of his nose with the back of his hand and listened to him exhale:

'Whoosh. Zippa-dee-fucking-doo-dah.'

Burgess began the next line with his second nostril. Okay, I'm gone, thought Junk, and stood. Burgess vacuumed a stray speck of dust off the desktop and looked up.

'Are you off? Well, right, blow their sweet little minds, eh?' Burgess said, holding his arm up as a salute. Junk nodded, Uh huh.

'Hey wait, look at this,' Burgess called Junk back a second. 'Is she lost?'

Junk looked at the monitor. A dark woman, well dressed in a designer suit, was passing by the security check. She seemed to be examining the airport-style metal detector as she walked through.

'What do you reckon she is, aside from being an alien element? Could she be a London journalist or something?' asked Burgess.

Junk said: 'Mm-mm, maybe.' She wasn't a reporter. There'd been no trouble near the Gravity for months. The Manchester/Gunchester angle had flattened out over the last few months. Unless something had happened that Junk hadn't heard about, which was always possible. Still, she wasn't a journalist.

Junk said, 'You don't know her, then?'

'No. Never seen her before. I'd say she's a journalist. Who knows, maybe we've won the Olympic bid and she's come to do a feature.' Burgess tapped out his rolled note, ready to scrape a new line together.

'Later,' said Junk, grabbing his satchel as he left. He couldn't believe it, he was the one with the dud eye. Even dressed as a woman, he was sure he knew who it was. Either he was fucked up, or Burgess was.

Estela had skipped the queue outside the Gravity by walking in with Cozy, who seemed to know everyone. She had passed by security without causing an incident, but was taken aback by the metal detectors on the doorway. England seemed a lot more gun-wise than she remembered. Checking her coat at the cloakroom, she had moved on to a room the size of an aircraft hangar.

She planned to stay with Cozy's crowd. She thought it was as good a way as any to find Yen. When Cozy said that they were heading downstairs, she had followed them to a dim bar below the dance floor.

'Is there a whole other floor down here?' she asked.

'No, just this bar. The rest of the basement is offices or powder rooms – restricted access,' said Cozy.

Cozy's friends were a mixed group, girls and boys, a couple of them black and one who was probably Pakistani. They were mixed but fairly homogeneous, ranging from fairly strung out by teenage angst and weekend drug-taking, to totally strung out and near total lunacy.

Estela eventually grew uncomfortable. It happened as she listened to a tiny blonde boy who believed in reincarnation. He wanted to talk about a drawing of a seventeenth-century shipwreck he once saw in a book. He said that he knew he'd been there in a past life. After seeing the picture, the whole scene had come back to him.

'It explained this dream I'd been having where I'm sat in bed, listening to my dad shouting. In front of me, there's this tunnel and I know my dad doesn't want me to go near it. But I go anyway. I get out of bed and start walking. The tunnel's really long and totally dark, but I know when I get to the end I'll find a door. When I open it I just step out and splash down into a pool of warm water.'

Estela wondered if she was the only one to be embarrassed, hearing this story. There was no way to shut the boy up.

'But then I get scared, I know something bad is about to happen. Suddenly, there's a shark. It's so close, I can feel its muscles brushing up against me. I know I'm going to die. But this hand comes down and pulls me out of the water. It's my dad again. He lifts me out of the water and saves me.'

Estela did not know whether to laugh or pretend not to be listening. She decided, instead, to ask a question.

'That proves you had a past life?'

'Yeah, because after I saw the picture in this book, I read what was written next to it. The sailors were eaten by sharks. I was reliving the experience. Actually living it over. If my dad hadn't intervened, I would have died.'

Another boy was nodding: 'It's clear, yeah. A classic case.'

'Classic,' Estela agreed. 'It's lucky your father happened to be passing.'

The blond boy looked close to tears. He didn't hear her. Estela thought, Jesus-Maria. Keep me away from him, he's about to go boom.

She decided to break with Cozy's crowd. When she caught up with Yen, it would anyway be better if she was alone with the thieving whore. Until then, she should get her bearings, also visit the bathroom and put her hosiery straight – later, perhaps find the time to bat her lashes at the cutest boy behind the bar. His eyes had looked to have a welcoming glint, when they had caught hers across the cellar. Although she suspected he might be a faggot.

She took one look at the queue outside the little girls' room, before thinking No Way, and marched purposefully into the boys'. Out of my way, this is a woman in a hurry.

Now she was upstairs again, she skirted around the edges of the dance floor and watched the crowds opening and folding around the solid beams of light and sonic bursts of discotic techno. She found the stairs and climbed to the balcony, looking for a panoramic grip on the excitement below.

The dance floor was solid with luminous bodies. On the podiums that punctured the mass of dancers, figures reared above the crowd, waving high above the floor. Along the front of the stage, dancers were grandstanding to the music, throwing gestures out into the viscous mix of sweat and sound.

The music descended to a low throb. Dry-ice was blasted into the dance floor, propelled by the giant fans attached to the underside of the balcony. Rumbling white clouds, stained by coloured lights, inflated until they filled the club. For a moment the dancers were obliterated. Then the music began to climb again and a figure burst through the clouds, dead centre, his arms outstretched in a crucifix, his long hair covered by a yellow sou'wester. The music reached 125 b.p.m. and the crowd let off aerosol-powered car horns, blowing whistles as they thumped their bodies. A resonant thrill of dense electricity charged the club. Estela felt it squeeze the breath right out of her body. She could use a drink.

Off to her right was a cocktail bar; she made for it. She

asked for a martini, turned from the bar, and saw Junk. He already had his eye on her. He must have been staring at her since she got to the bar. Jesus, he was a fright. She would have sworn that he had the evil eye, the kind that men believed could shrivel your balls with a glance. He had the right angle for the view: sat eye-level with her crotch now she had turned to meet him. His monocular gaze travelled up Estela's body, across her breasts, her falling neckline and high neck, and settled around her face. Estela flatly returned his stare:

'Ooh, you are ugly. You could turn Our Lady's milk sour,' she said.

'I know you, don't I?' said Junk.

'In your dreams,' said Estela. 'But nowhere else, piss-eye.'

Junk held up his hands: 'I wasn't trying anything. Just: do I know you?'

'You were looking me over pretty assiduously; now you don't know if you seen me before or not?'

Junk said, 'I've seen you before. I saw you come in the club. But have I seen you before that?'

'Have you?'

'No, I don't think so. I never forget a face. I walk into walls because my depth perception is shot, but I never forget a face. You must have reminded me of someone,' said Junk. 'Do you want to sit?'

Estela sat. 'You been playing I-spy with your one little eye since the moment I walked into this place?'

'I caught sight of you on a security monitor.'

She said, 'You're part of security? I would have thought that you were the element that security was trying to combat. Are you a double agent?'

'I'm staff,' said Junk. He held out his hand, 'My name's John.'

'Estela Santos.' She took his hand.

'Are you Spanish?' Junk asked.

'Brazilian.'

'Is that a Brazilian name?'

'No, it's Spanish,' admitted Estela. 'I have mixed blood.'

Estela drained her glass down to the olive and set it down. Junk took the hint, and stood: 'Martini?'

'Gin and French.'

When Junk returned, Estela asked him what kind of staff he was. Creative, non combative, he said. He had an invalidity pension and a little room above the dance floor where he could pass his days in peace.

'So what do you do?' asked Estela

'You've seen the screens either side of the stage, above the dance floor?' Estela nodded. 'I put the pictures up there.'

'Why are you not doing that now?'

'My assistant can handle it. I'll drop by later – when her and Yen go off and dance.'

Estela heard the name: 'Yen?'

'Yeah, her boyfriend.'

Estela stood, turned and she was straight out of the cocktail bar. She had passed three cabins as she walked along the balcony. Yen was in one of them. She had him.

She pushed open the first door, a fat DJ looked up at her: 'Yeah?' She slammed the door shut immediately. Junk was running behind her now, calling out: 'What's the problem? Hey. Hey, qué pasa?'

Estela ignored him; she passed over the two boys in the lighting room and was making for the third door. A girl was hurtling towards her, mouth open, almost pushing Estela over as she charged along the balcony. Junk only just saved Estela from falling. He was right on top of her, shouting, 'Estela? Estela? Theresa?'

Estela had her hand on the door; pushing it open, she saw Yen lying on the floor. His neck was shot open, his eyes open towards the ceiling, the back of his head dissolving into a mess of blood.

Junk was at the door now: 'Jesus. Jesus. Jesus. Fuck. Fuck.'

Estela turned away from Yen. Junk was behind her, filling the doorway. If she leapt now, he would collapse. She could knock him out of the way and be out of the club – but she didn't believe it was her wisest move. She was stuck, she would have to stay. She was probably on video anyway: walking towards the room, walking into the room, walking somewhere in the general area, scene-of-the-crime. If she was on video, would that clear her of the killing? There was no way that time-of-death could clear her – the blood was still pumping out of the poor slut.

There were people behind Junk now. He was attracting a crowd. She could see faces, trying to peer around him. She heard someone scream. She was trapped, no question. She turned again, away from Yen's corpse and away from Junk. She could still hear him muttering behind her: 'Jesus, Jesus, Fuck, Jesus.' Too right – Jesus-fuck-Maria, she thought. She leant her hands against the editing desk and peered through the window at the dancers below. What a mess. If she kept her head, well maybe, okay perhaps, but only if she kept her head. Just so long as she could not be tied to the killing. If it was her gun, well, no one could prove it was her gun.

Where was the gun?

Estela turned; the door was full of faces now. Leaning, craning, peering. Junk was on his knees by the corpse. Estela saw him holding the nickel-plated Beretta with a piece of his shirt, shielding himself from the crowd as he wiped the gun clean. Then he dropped it on to the floor, into the spreading pool of blood.

SEVEN

Estela drank her coffee white with sugar; the policewoman took the order and moved smoothly off, as though she rode on castors. The hum of the fans from the microprocessors, xerox machines and printers was oddly comforting, like insects on a warm evening. She knew that, outside the door, the line of people to be interviewed stretched along the length of two corridors. She was special, though; she had been the first person on the scene and she was being waited upon separately. Along with Junk, who was already being interviewed in a closed room.

Estela had already passed through a preliminary interview. She had filled out forms, she had produced her passport and answered questions on her stay in England. She had briefly recounted the story of how she found Yen's body. She had been walking along the back of the balcony, a door was flung open, someone – a youth – had rushed past her. Through the open door she saw a body, and she saw the blood. No, she did not recognise the youth who had pushed past her. No, she did not know the dead boy. That was all she knew. Yes, she was happy to wait and answer further questions. Yes, she understood they were very busy. Yes, three sugars, please.

And now Junk was alone in an interview room. She trusted him, to an extent. She believed her chances to be good, for the moment. The truth would not come out immediately. While Estela and Junk had waited together for the police, three hours ago now, she had made him understand her version of events.

'Listen, John. I don' know Yen and I wasn't looking for him. I saw his body by chance, only because I was passing when that girl pushed past me. That is my story; if you have a different version then I will recall other details: like seeing you wipe the gun.'

Junk had seemed to weigh the proposition, then had said: 'Forget it was a girl you saw. A figure rushed past you. All right?'

That was fine, then. What did it matter, anyway, boy/girl – it wasn't as though gender was set in stone. She sipped at her coffee and watched while the two detectives strode towards her along a blue-white corridor.

'Miss Santos, if we could have a word now,' they said, or one of them said – the other tacked a 'thank you' on to the end.

Estela followed them into a square room, with a cheap formica desk at the centre. They resumed their questions, consulting sheets of typed papers. Estela could see her name written across the top of one.

'You are visiting England on business . . . You represent a Brazilian record company specialising in Latin American music in general . . . You will be attending the Manchester Festival of World Music Dance Drama.'

Estela nodded between each sentence, making an 'mm-mm' sound to emphasise her acquiescence on the tape. The detective continued: 'Your current address is 5c Palatine Court, Withington . . . You are renting the flat off a Mr Mark Whittam who is currently on holiday in New York . . . His flat was advertised in an English magazine, you do not know Mr Whittam personally . . . Your accommodation was arranged through the offices of your company in Brazil. . . . I'm sorry, through an English record company that's involved in a joint venture with your own company.'

'That is right, officer.' That was her story.

'Your visa is in order,' said one of the detectives. Estela could not tell whether this was a question or a statement. She remained silent and they did not ask her to speak up.

'You found the body of John Caxton at eleven thirty p.m.,' the detectives continued, their heads turned down to the A4 sheets that lay on the desk. Estela began to realise she could not tell one from the other. The bland bureaucracy of the English police was beginning to hypnotise her.

'You found the body of John Caxton at eleven thirty p.m.'

Estela said, 'I did not check the time. Nor do I know the name of the poor boy that I found, when I found him.'

'Thank you,' one of the detectives looked up at her. Estela sat, she stared at the detective before realising that her interview had ended, her evidence assimilated.

'Thank you,' the detective repeated, holding a pen out to her. The other detective swivelled a sheet of paper around on the desktop so that its foot rested by Estela's hand. She took the pen and signed her name.

As she left, a detective told her they would probably call on her again at her Withington address – she had no plans to leave? Estela assured them that she had not. She was to remain in Manchester for another two weeks. She wondered, privately, whether she should not run now. While her story and her cover remained plausible.

Estela calculated that she had two days, perhaps, before she was re-questioned. One of Yen's friends would mention having seen her, she believed. She had looked over the faces of the other witnesses, the ones that had been left waiting on another corridor while her evidence was taken. None of them was familiar. She might count on two days' grace. She could complete her job and disappear.

If she could complete her job, then she could disappear

– she corrected herself. There was now a whole wall of interference between herself and Burgess; she risked static whether she completed the hit immediately or whether she waited. For her own sweet peace, she would have to find out why the past days had blown without harmony. She could almost believe someone was unhinging her constellation. The influence of Saturn on her house could not be discounted. Standing in the reception area of a police station, she was alone with the smell of an industrial cleaning agent. The whole building was spotless. She had never associated law enforcement and hygiene before – she must be growing old. She began pressing at a bell-button on the reception counter. When a policeman appeared, she asked him to call her a taxi – she was about to drop.

'Two taxis,' Junk appeared behind her. 'They've done with me, for now.'

Estela said, 'You want to share a cab.'

'Where are you going?'

'Withington.'

'No, I'm heading north,' said Junk. 'Tottington.'

'Yes?'

When the first taxi arrived, Estela took it but asked the driver to pull around the corner and wait. She was going to follow Junk. At the moment his cab reached the Stockport road, she knew that she had made the right move. Tottington sounded implausible.

Theresa was sitting in darkness, huddled on a spindly chair in a corner of her kitchen. Junk entered through the back yard and tapped at the kitchen door. Theresa heard him whispering his name and hers. She pulled back the bolt, let him through and went back to her little seat. What had happened? What had happened? She wasn't sure whether she asked him or he asked her.

'Yen's dead,' said Junk.

She knew that.

'What happened?' he asked again.

She had shot him. What now?

Theresa imagined a white chalk mark drawn around a bare floor and a body in a drawer, wrapped in a polythene sleeping bag, the zipper running from toe to crown. Whatever remained of the crown, afterwards. She saw policemen in blue anoraks tracing imaginary lines at a murder scene. A piece of cotton tied around a pin and drawn tight to indicate the trajectory the bullet took from the gun, as she held it. She saw the bullet leave the gun again, rip through Yen and leave a bloody stain on the wall, six feet above and behind the spot where he had been standing. She saw Yen on the floor, his throat punched through. When she knelt beside him and took his head in her hand, there had been a hole – just at the spot where his cranium had once bulged. She looked up; there are his brains, all of them. She looked up; Junk was pleading with her: 'Tréz, Tréz, what happened?'

'I pointed a gun at him and it went off,' she said.

'Where did the gun come from, Theresa?'

'Nowhere, it came out of the air.'

Junk crouched down beside her. 'Oh, Theresa. How could it have? How could it have? Theresa, Theresa.'

He guessed that she was in shock. She must be in shock. He couldn't believe she had killed Yen deliberately, and he couldn't explain the gun. He knelt down close to her chair. He held her hands.

'Theresa, did Yen bring the gun? Was it his gun?'

After he'd visited the Taz-Man, Junk had hooked up with Yen and Theresa. They had all gone to the Gravity together. Although it was early, the security team had already arrived. Perhaps they hadn't had chance to turn the metal detectors on. If the metal detectors weren't working, then Yen could have smuggled a gun past the bouncers. But perhaps the gun was already inside the club, hidden somewhere. Yen had visited them at the club that afternoon. He may have found the gun in Burgess's office. If that was where the gun came from, then he was better off dead. Junk knew what Yen was like, that he would steal anything. Junk should never have taken him downstairs.

'Was the gun Yen's? . . . Did he bring it with him? . . . Or was it Burgess's? . . . Theresa, listen, did Yen steal one of Burgess's guns? . . . Did he? . . . Please, please, Tréz,' he pleaded with her.

Because she remained silent, Junk fell silent.

They were still in the dark when Estela let herself in, flicking on the light as she passed through the kitchen door.

'Hello, Junk,' she said. 'Why don't you put the kettle on and introduce me to your friend?'

Junk didn't react, didn't even curse her for following him.

He just looked her over, slowly. Until, standing at last, he said, 'Theresa, this is Paul Sorel. Paul, Theresa O'Donnell.'

EIGHT

Estela made the tea, scalding the pot and setting it down on the kitchen table with a half-turn to agitate the water. The milk stood in a gravy boat, there was no jug anywhere. She had found a clean teaspoon but sugared and stirred everyone's tea without asking how they preferred it. The three of them sat around the kitchen table and drank the pot dry. Estela believed the extra-sweet tea would help to ease Theresa out of shock, but the girl had not said a word so far. Junk and Estela talked. Junk called her Paul once but she stopped him: 'It's Estela.'

'I thought you'd call yourself Lola if you ever went through with the operation.'

Estela said no. 'Too obvious.'

'I meant The Raincoats version, not the Kinks.'

Estela liked the way Junk could forget whole reams of things that anyone else might remember but never forget that she had loved a cover song by The Raincoats. Could it be transposed to flamenco, she wondered. She looked at Junk's ill-matched eyes, the real one far spacier than its partner. He said he recognised her immediately he saw her. He said, 'I like your new accent.'

'It's irreversible.' The Manchester accent disappeared along with her Adam's apple.

'Why are you back?'

'It was supposed to be a holiday. I planned to pass through town like a ghost. But when I walked into that bar and saw the photograph of John Burgess staring back at me, I knew something would go wrong. Was it you who sent Yen over to talk to me? That was bad luck for both of us.'

Yen hadn't needed much persuasion. When Junk told her that, he could tell she was flattered. Her voice fluttered. But as she leant closer to Junk, she dropped a quarter-octave: 'This girl killed Yen, didn't she?'

Junk was almost positive: 'She was alone with him, so what else could have happened? She says the gun just appeared, but Yen must have took it from Burgess's office – where else could it come from?'

'Where else? Don' ask me. I hear everyone in Manchester carries a gun, nowadays.'

They weren't uncommon. The more Junk visited the Taz-Man, the more guns he saw. But Yen would never have had one.

Estela improvised: 'You think no? Thanks to you, I knew him. He was a thief and a dealer. All his talk – it was about the big deals he was planning, the money he was going to make.'

Junk knew this sounded wrong. Even if Yen was dealing, he'd be doing ten tabs here, ten tabs there. 'He'd be doing it in clubs, where the bouncers keep out the lunatics and the police warn off the gangs. He was a clubhead, a face, he knew everyone and everyone knew him. Why would he need a gun?'

Estela had a new argument. 'He would deal on credit. He was no Vatican banker. Suppose he lost a few tabs each week. Say, he was too stoned to remember where he hid them, or he gave too many away. Or he took them all himself. He might end owing thousands to some really nasty men. Don' tell me he wouldn't want some kind of protection.'

Junk knew Yen wasn't the type, not at all. Why bother to flesh out the whole bare, sad mystery? He said, 'Yen was in Burgess's office a few hours before he died. We both know Burgess loves guns, so why look for a drugs angle? Leave that to the police. Once they open Yen up, they'll identify traces of insecticide on a tomato he ate last year, they're so hyped for a new drugs story.'

Estela wouldn't give up. 'Why is it not a drugs story? If the gun belongs to Burgess, perhaps Burgess is the wholesaler. Half the kids I meet are teetotal. If Burgess ran drugs inside his club, whatever he loses at the bar he could make back on chemicals.'

'No.'

'Tell me: why no, Junk? Tell me?' Estela stared Junk out, her voice tuned to an interrogative key. 'All that security, what's that for? I tell you: for one reason. To keep accredited dealers safe. A policy of containment, pure and simple. I'm Latin American – I know these things.'

'Burgess isn't involved with drugs,' said Junk. He was sure. 'He's got a heavy coke habit, yeah. I know because I'm the one who gets the stuff for him. But he's so far out of the business, he can't even score for himself.'

Estela knew Burgess could not be clean. That would make no sense. If Héctor Barranco Garza wanted him dead, he had to be involved in something. She kept pushing: 'Why would Burgess need guns if he's an honest businessman?'

'He's straight, he might be honest. But he's still a total whacked-out psychopath.'

'I was beginning to think he had changed beyond recognition,' said Estela, giving up. 'It's good to be home again. I'll put the kettle on. I love the Americas, but I had forgotten what a real cup of tea tasted like.'

The kitchen lay at the back of a terraced house, an old two up/two down. The linoleum looked like an original fixture; worn to a pitted pink, it echoed lightly beneath Estela's heels as she hustled round the hob. Turning the spent teabags into the sink, Estela was thinking, Jesus-Maria, how to get an angle on this whole mess. As the kettle began to whistle, she was telling herself that this was all she needed: a kitchen-sink drama. What should she try next?

'I've given you three sugars,' she told Theresa. 'Believe me, it is exactly what you need.'

Sugar was supposed to feed the brain. Was this girl as stupid as Yen – had she just picked up a strange gun and shot the boy?

She said, 'What did you say about the police? That they are certain to cut him open?'

'I guess so.'

Estela could guess what drugs they would find. She tried a last strategy.

'Why are you so sure it's an accident? The girl was the one who shot him, she probably had her reasons.'

Junk stared at Estela: she must know she was wrong. She must feel it. She had always been able to catch the nuances in a situation. Even as a boy, she had a woman's intuition. He wouldn't have believed it, but perhaps that part of her was all dried out.

She saw the look but carried on. 'Perhaps the girl was jealous. She's only young, she don' have my experience. Maybe the boy told her how good I was. Maybe he described the look on my face as he fucked me in the mouth.'

Junk could not deal with that one. He couldn't throw it back. He couldn't even look at her. It would be too obvious that his brain was buzzing, trying to see past her expression to work out if she were telling the truth. He reddened and looked away.

Theresa saved him. Her voice was just audible but it got through to him. 'It was her gun. Yen said he found it in her case, after she passed out.'

Junk turned on Estela. 'Of course, it was your gun.' He saw it now.

Theresa's voice was limping but was not unfirm. 'Yen was playing with it. I asked him if it was real. He said it couldn't be, it felt like a toy. It was lightweight and the handle was hollow. Even if it was real, it didn't work.'

Her voice finally seized.

Estela finished the scene. 'There was no magazine, but there was one bullet in the chamber. You found the safety catch and flicked it off without realising. That's how you shot him.'

Theresa wailed. Estela covered Theresa's hands with her own and then, as the tears began to pour, took Theresa in her arms and mothered her. She could not stop the noise but she did not even try. She just held Theresa, and let her weep on her shoulder until they were both damp.

Junk lit the gas fire in the parlour. They had wrapped Theresa in a duvet and let her doze on the settee. Estela continued to hold her. Junk sat opposite in a tatty armchair. Dawn was beginning to bleed through the sheet that had been nailed over the window as a makeshift curtain. Junk rolled a joint, either as a nightcap or as breakfast.

He said, 'Are you in a hurry to head back?'

Estela said, 'Not so great a hurry. I'll see what I can do here first.'

'I think you should.'

He handed her the joint. Estela thought she would be unable to stomach English dope, but the smoke overtook her on her tired side and she relaxed into it. The last thing she remembered, Junk asked if she had come to kill Burgess. It was true, but it was not the way he imagined.

She told him: 'No.' Transsexuals have a curiously pacific psychological profile, did he not know anything?

Why did she have a gun, then? Well, a girl has got to have protection.

NINE

Junk walked out of Levenshulme into morning light that was equal parts silver and ash. The rain had slowed to almost nothing, just hazy spray in the air. He caught a bus halfway to Hulme along Wilbraham Road and walked the rest. He thought he would be better on his own – get his head together. Mornings like these seemed to graze the old scars along his cheeks, to pepper his skin like alcohol. An ashy silver morning could invigorate him better than the saunas, the swims, the vitamin drinks he used to wake himself up – now that he hardly ever slept.

Closer to Hulme, the pulpy smell from the brewery had already begun to dull the morning's edge. Junk crossed over a patch of green where the pit bulls played, and climbed the steps at Elmin Walk, up to his flat. The door was open and he could hear his own television playing inside. He walked through.

The front room was full of men in dinner jackets, black bow ties and Crombie great-coats. It looked like a bouncers' convention, all of them sat around watching as the weather-girl pointed at another area of rain-bearing pressure, moving in from the Atlantic. Bernard was the biggest and the oldest, sat apart on Junk's only chair. His boys were gathered around him: Billy leant against a wall, Frank and John on the floor. They all looked up as Junk walked into his own room.

Bernard said, 'All right, John Quay. We been waiting up all fucking night.'

'Sorry, Big Lad. I would have rushed home sooner,' said Junk.

'Well, let's not hang about any more. We'd best get going.'

There was no question, Junk just turned right around and walked back out with them. If he had wanted to do one, he should have run the minute he saw they were waiting for him. But he knew that he would have to speak to Burgess soon. It was better to get it over and done. If he disappeared for a day or two, Bernard would tell his boys to leave Junk's door open, let anyone walk in and steal what they wanted – that would teach Junk to fanny about.

Junk said, 'Leave the telly on. It's better if people think I'm in. And lock up behind you.'

'Okay John, anything you say.' Bernard pulled on the chain that hung in a loop from his trouser pocket. At the other end was a great bunch of keys. Bernard re-locked Junk's door, elaborately fastening all three locks, the Yale and the deadlocks at the top and bottom.

'It's not what you'd call a good neighbourhood, eh?'

'It's all right.' Junk shrugged. He had steel sheets on the window, the door was reinforced. The flat was larger than anything else he could afford, a maisonette flat built for a family of four or five, only two minutes' walk from the town centre. And, he could have added, there was still a neighbourhood feel – although there were some in the neighbourhood who would rob their own grandmothers, they were in the minority.

Junk had bought his locks off Burgess, who told him he happened to have a few spare deadlocks after a re-fit at home. Burgess had said, 'Go on and take them, it saves you forty pounds.' Junk knew Burgess would keep a set of keys for himself. But why argue? If it satisfied Burgess's paranoia, it meant a quieter life for him. Burgess could have the door kicked in any time he wanted, anyway.

'Where is Burgess?' asked Junk. 'At the club or at his place?'

'He'll be back home by now; he said that if we couldn't find you by four then we should head out to the ranch.'

That was it, then. A half hour drive down to Knutsford with Bernard and his boys. Unless Bernard decided to let Billy, Frank and John get off home to bed. They must have been sat waiting in his front room all night.

Just two seconds later, as they crossed towards the big black Lexus SL400, Bernard dismissed his boys. Junk felt like he was getting lucky. At least he could ride down in comfort instead of being squashed on a back seat between two eighteen-stoners. The only problem was having to put up with Bernard's good humour. Junk liked comedians to be cheerful; he preferred it if thugs were dour.

Bernard's Lexus had central-locking. Junk would get fair warning if he was going to get thrown out on the motorway. As the door studs clicked into place, an old soul record cranked up on the car stereo: 'There's A Ghost In My House' by R. Dean Taylor. Bernard sang along. After ten minutes, Junk realised it was a CD, programmed to repeat the same track over and over. He tried to blot it out.

They were out in the countryside when Bernard broke off mid-verse and said, 'How did the coppers treat you, John?'

This was it. Junk tried to keep it level, off-hand or off the top of his head. 'No worries. Fine.'

'Who was that bird they took away with you?'

'A tourist. From Brazil.'

Bernard said, 'I had a Brazilian once. She was all right.'

Junk had had these kind of chats before. Bernard reckoned to have shagged everyone in the world.

'I had a couple of Venezuelans once. I tell you, they were a pair of Caracas – I saw fireworks.'

Junk nodded. Uh-huh, nice one, big lad.

'So what could you tell the coppers, owt or nowt? I tell you, I can't fucking believe it. We've spent a fortune on all this hi-tech airport-stylie Israeli security gear and someone sails through and blasts the throat out of some kid. You wouldn't credit it, would you.'

Junk said, 'I've no idea what happened.'

'And what the fuck was he doing in your room? I tell you, it's a fucking mystery, that's all I can say. I bet the coppers are going mental,' Bernard said.

'I don't know, Bernard. I don't know how he got in my room.'

'Of course, it's all on video, so Burgess should be able to tell us exactly what went down.'

There would be something on a security video. Junk couldn't lie outright to Burgess without knowing what Burgess had learnt from the tapes. The door to his room had been shut, so there would be no film of the actual shooting. Junk had been trying to remember exactly where the camera stood in relation to his room. As far as he could think, it looked down the length of the balcony. Burgess could have a picture of Theresa entering and leaving the room. In fact, that was all he could have, but that was about as bad as anything. Junk didn't see how he could keep Theresa out of it. There was no clear way of keeping her out at all.

'Oh yeah, it'll all be on video,' Junk said, keeping calm as he spoke. 'Open and shut. Burgess has given the tapes to the police by now, I suppose.'

Bernard said, 'Strange thing. There's about a hundred fucking coppers in the place, and none of them thinks to ask for the video tapes. I tell you, I don't know what we pay fucking taxes for – all the money that goes to the police, it's a crying shame. What I'd like to see, right, is performance-related pay. They catch a villain, they get paid. Otherwise, nothing. They have to send their missus out on the streets to make up the short-fall.' Bernard was gloating. 'I had a copper's wife once. She was all right.'

Junk kept quiet the rest of the way to Knutsford. As they rolled up the drive towards Burgess's house, the pack of Dobermanns and Akitas kept pace with Bernard's car. Junk kept his eyes ahead, trying to figure out his best strategy, any strategy. He still had no idea when they reached the door and met Burgess. He could tell Burgess was in an evil temper.

'Junk, get your arse down here.' Burgess turned on his heels and strode down the corridor.

There was nothing for Junk to say. He dropped his head and followed Burgess across the hallway. What now?

Burgess's house was split-level, built in the seventies. Junk thought of it as Tracey Island, it had that style of low roof and glass exterior, all of it put together on the flat open plan Junk associated with Thunderbirds or Captain Scarlett. Walking by the indoor pool, he always expected the water to slide away and a rocket to fire through Burgess's gently pitched roof. There was no chance of Junk seeing the pool today, unless he was tied to the bottom.

Burgess walked as far as the kitchen and stopped. Holding out his arm he pointed Junk in the direction of his office: 'Get in there.'

Junk didn't like walking ahead of Burgess, feeling his eyes behind him. At least Bernard seemed to have disappeared.

Burgess opened the door on to his home office. The TV inside was tuned to the video channel. Its screen glowed blue in anticipation.

'Sit down,' said Burgess.

Junk sat in view of the TV. From somewhere behind his head, Burgess flicked with the remote control and the tape started running. On the screen was a picture of Junk, walking through the door of the Gravity alongside Yen and Theresa. Yen was playing around, skipping to the side, laughing. Behaving the way he always did, like an idiot. Junk looked at the image of himself, watching as he nodded 'hi' to Billy the Bouncer and walked through the upright columns on the metal detector. What he hadn't seen at the time, because he was ahead of Yen, was Yen skip around the outside of the metal detector. He wouldn't have thought anything of it if he had noticed at the time; it was only Yen being funny, acting-up as he always did. But now that he knew that Yen was carrying Estela's gun, the little skip had become weighty, significant. Did Yen know the gun was real? The prat, dancing around but already one of the walking fucking dead.

'That's the dead boy, isn't it?' said Burgess. 'John Caxton.'

Junk looked up, surprised. He had only heard Yen's real name once before, and that was in the police station.

'Yeah, John Caxton.'

'What's he doing with you?'

Junk said, 'I just know him. I met up with him outside.'

'Well, he works for me,' said Burgess. 'And now he's wound up shot in my club. How the fuck do you reckon that looks?'

'He works for you?' Junk was confused. 'What does he do? I know everyone in that place.'

'He doesn't work at the Grav, he works at my travel agents, in town. He's one of those cunts who sits in front of a VDU all day, flogging package tours to the Greek Islands.'

'He's got a day job?' Junk had never thought about it,

he never supposed that Yen worked. Yen was a natural slacker. Junk had assumed that he slept all day.

'Yeah, he works for me,' Burgess was keeping it suppressed, but he was near-boiling. 'What I don't figure – how is it one of my employees ends up shot inside one of my clubs? How does it look?'

Junk didn't know. How did it look? Like the slightest of coincidences, who would care? – but Burgess clearly thought there was more to it.

'Why was he in your room?' asked Burgess.

'I let him open up for me. He was just waiting until I got back from that chat I was having with you,' said Junk. It's all he could think to say.

'The kid behind him,' said Burgess as he hit Rewind. Junk saw Yen dance backwards around the security unit. 'Who's she?'

This was it, and Yen couldn't lie. Everyone at the Gravity knew that Theresa was Junk's assistant.

'Theresa. She's the one who introduced me to John Caxton. She helps me out, playing the videos if I have to step outside.'

'Yeah? Well, look at this.' Burgess crossed the room and switched the tapes. The new tape showed the balcony. This is it, thought Junk.

'Look there,' said Burgess. He used a biro to point at the screen.

Junk saw Theresa from a distance. The video could have been clearer, but despite the fuzzy definition and the number of other figures walking along the balcony, Junk knew it was her. He watched as she walked towards Junk's video booth; she opened the door.

'She stays in there for less than half a minute,' said Burgess. 'Look.'

Burgess put the tape on fast forward, the figures on the balcony moved around on frenetic legs, speeding through a ten-second skank. As Burgess stabbed the Play button again, Junk saw himself and Estela coming along the balcony. Estela was ahead of him, opening the doors to the DJ booth and the lighting room next to it. As Estela got to the door of the video booth, Theresa barged out, collided with Estela, then turned and fled.

'You and the tourist weren't the first on the scene, this Theresa girl was,' said Burgess, tapping at the TV screen. 'What I want, is for you to get her and bring her to me. I want to speak to her before the cops – have you got that? She talks to me, or you lose the other fucking eye.'

'Yeah, okay.' Junk was confused.

'You know where to find her?' asked Burgess.

'Theresa?'

'Yeah, Theresa.'

Junk nodded, uh-huh.

He didn't know how to explain what he'd seen on the tape. All he could think was that Theresa had left the room in a panic after she had shot Yen, but returned, almost immediately. Perhaps to recheck the body. He had to ask: 'If you have all that on the video, don't you have the killer?'

'That's the beginning of the video. That camera had only just started recording. Someone had taken the video tape for this camera out of the machine. I'd only just found out.'

That had been Junk's fault. When he'd shown Theresa his latest tape, he had used Burgess's security equipment. He must have forgotten to put the blank tape back into the machine. It was lucky, he supposed. All he said was: 'Let's see it again.'

Burgess played the first few minutes of the tape through again. There was no doubt that it was Theresa. There was no mistaking her, not if you knew her – not even if you had only seen her once before. But all the video showed was her walking into the room, waiting, and coming out again. She might have shot Yen inside those few seconds, but she would have had to be quick.

Looking at it a third time, Junk could see that Theresa's hands were empty and all she was wearing was a too-short T-shirt and tight black trousers. There was no way she was carrying a gun at that moment. Junk risked asking: 'What do you think happened, boss?'

'Fucked if I know. She goes in, she must see a blood spattered corpse and so she just does one, flits.'

'And there's no way she would have stayed around to meet the cops,' said Junk. He had an idea, now. He couldn't see quite how it might help, but it would confuse the picture. It would worry Burgess for sure. 'There's no way she'd want to talk to the cops after Caxton was killed. It would come out about his drug dealing.'

Burgess was looking pale. 'John Caxton is a dealer?'

'Yeah. Your dealer. When I buy a couple of grammes for you, it's him that I get it off. That's why he was in my room, he was just sorting his kit out – you know, folding up some wraps so he could flog them throughout the night.'

Burgess smashed his fist into Junk's face. Junk saw it coming, but just sat there. He took the follow-up full-on.

Burgess screamed, 'You fucking moron. I should have you fucking killed. I should have Bernard throw you to the fucking dogs, a fucking T-bone rammed up your arse. You let a coke dealer sort out his wraps in my club. What do you think the bouncers are for, all this fucking Jew security. I'm supposed to be clean. I'm running a straight club, I'm through with fucking drug dens.'

'I did him a favour,' said Junk, sniffling through the blood that caked his nose. 'He did me a favour, getting all the coke you want – you know, like you told me: good quality, none of this baby-powder shit.'

'You arsehole. You really fucking fried your brains back in the seventies, didn't you. The reason you get the coke is so no one finds me rooting around with drug dealers,' shouted Burgess. 'What's the fucking point if you bring the scum into the club?'

'I screwed up,' said Junk. This was it now, the line that would really shake Burgess: 'But I can't see it matters. You said he worked for you, so no matter where he dies, it gets linked back to you.'

Junk knew he had saved Theresa from the police. If Burgess had been so worried about being linked with a dead boy, he'd be a thousand times more anxious not to be linked with a dead drug dealer. He would make sure no one spoke to Theresa, so long as he believed Theresa could tie him into some drug scam. Perhaps make it look as though he still kept a string of dealers running out of his clubs and bars – just like the old days.

The only worry, now: Burgess might make sure Theresa never spoke to the police, or anyone else.

TEN

Estela woke, still wrapped around Theresa, hugging her inside a lemon duvet. She had to twist Theresa's head to free her arm and look at her wristwatch. She did not like what she saw: a quarter to eleven. She was getting to be a heavy sleeper, although she could only have had three or four hours in total. She felt dull and flat, she wanted her hormone tablets and she wanted them now. Damn that slut Yen. The poor boy. Estela disentangled herself from Theresa and looked around for her handbag. She knew that she had emergency items of make-up. What she needed was her complete vanity kit, but she could never return to the apartment. She would have to make do with whatever she could find.

Theresa was deep in sleep. Estela decided that a complete interrogation could wait. First she would look around the girl's bathroom and see what kind of skin care products she kept. After a glance around Theresa's mis-kept home, Estela was not prepared to bet on a lavishly stocked bathroom. Theresa hardly needed full-scale cosmetic enhancement, anyway. Asleep, she was such a slight thing. Estela liked her face. The down-turned mouth made her appear both serious and shrewd. She was certainly pretty. Estela might have paid good money for those eyelashes.

The steep, narrow and dark stairs ended opposite a bathroom that was nearer to being clean than filthy. The tiny window above the lavatory was chock full of cleansers and toners, most of them wrapped in decorative wicker baskets, as though Christmas had just passed and every one of Theresa's aunts had decided to go with soaps-and-smells. Theresa was a Catholic name. She must have a thousand aunties. Estela looked over all the little plastic bottles. They would be fine if she was making a jello salad but she was not going to put any of them on her skin: passion fruit shampoo, banana moisturiser, aubergine (or egg-plant) cleansing milk, thyme and sea-weed eye balm. Estela could not guess what kind of criminally insane hippie would have supplied this poisonous goo.

A range of Clinique toners and moisturisers stood by the sink. Estela found them eventually. Within a half-hour, she had all but completed a makeshift facial and could begin to get dressed again. She decided to put a tight and wide elastic hairband across the top of her forehead, holding back her thick black hair and pulling the flesh of her face up in the surprised fox/Joan Collins style. She finished by dabbing perfume in the shadowy crescents underneath her breasts. She thanked God and Our-Lady-of-lactation that they were still beautiful. She had not even begun to lose her figure. A seventeen year old would risk damnation for breasts like hers.

Her glamour restored, she returned downstairs, detouring through the kitchen before she woke Theresa. While she fed the toaster, Estela tuned the radio/cassette on the worktop to Piccadilly Radio. She guessed that she'd missed the local news. But perhaps a little music would get some signs of life out of the Theresa-shaped duvet. After spluttering through an ad for exhaust pipes, the radio surfaced with the first bars of Blondie's 'Heart of Glass'. Estela had to stop and wait for Debbie Harry's vocals to begin. How could anyone invent a voice like that? The sullen sublime. It wasn't until the song ended, and the DJ gave the dates, that Estela remembered the song was thirteen years old. It was a summer hit; it must have been playing somewhere the night she left Manchester. She had once had a Debbie Harry wig. It was lost on the night she was arrested. The desk sergeant had taken it and logged it in his big black book, along with her purse, stiletto shoes and her season ticket for Manchester City. She never got any of them back.

Estela put her mind back on breakfast. After a while, she went to wake Theresa, honeying the tones and velvetting the Latin cadences as she whispered 'darling? darling?' She would have made an excellent extra aunty.

Theresa's eyelashes swung open on clear blue eyes. As the girl focused, Estela thought she saw semi-circular lines swivel beneath the Celtic glaze, reminding her of the telescopic sightfinder on cameras and rifles.

'I put on the kettle, darling,' said Estela. She stroked Theresa's hair out of her eyes, revealing a bony porcelain forehead with a single crack running across it. Theresa had woken unhappily.

The toast was ready. Estela had found a tub of crumb-filled margarine in the fridge, but no butter. The margarine congealed in pools on the slabs of white toast that Theresa couldn't eat. Estela wondered if she should try and persuade the girl to eat something, but didn't bother. As they sat together, Theresa began to worry that the fire had been on too long. Estela told her not to be silly and took a ten pound note out of her purse.

'I'll pay. I don' want either of us to freeze.'

Theresa took the money. She asked Estela how she had come to know Junk.

'I once lived in Manchester,' Estela told her. Estela had intended keeping the truth to a minimum, but did not know how carefully Theresa had listened to her conversation with Junk. If Junk chose, he could tell Theresa everything anyway. 'I was born here.'

'It doesn't sound like it, that's all I can say.' Theresa had the urban nasal slur of a Manchester girl. Estela thought: north Manchester; Blackley, certainly no further from town than Crumpsall.

Estela said: 'Was Yen your boyfriend?'

Theresa's mouth took another down turn, but she held on to her tears: 'No, he was a friend.'

The duvet had begun to slip off Theresa's pale shoulders. Estela tucked it around the girl as though she had been born to play her mother. 'Tell me, what did Yen say about me exactly?'

Theresa's voice had a sour edge. 'About finding a gun at your place? He said you had photographs of John Burgess and a gun. He joked that you were planning to knock him off, but there's no other explanation. It was a real gun.'

'A nine millimetre Beretta, it was a very good piece. Now the police have it, and I am helpless.' Estela hoped that her lip had quivered.

'Not as helpless as Yen.'

'No? We can pray for him. I don' have a prayer unless I find another gun,' said Estela. 'I was not intending to kill Burgess but if he finds me, then I prefer to get to him first.'

Only Theresa's head was visible above the duvet, her little face and large Irish eyes. Could Estela really kill Burgess?

Estela said, 'You have to understand, Burgess is mad. Not just loopy, he is mad at me because I once caused him a certain amount of emotional pain.'

Estela paused. She last saw Burgess the night she had broken out of prison. Burgess had looked in pain, certainly. He was lying on the floor, his hands over his face. As she stepped over him and walked to the door, he seemed to be crying.

'I know Burgess and I know the way his mind works. He's the kind who thinks too intensely. He barely sleeps, which gives him too much time to brood. He wants revenge. If I don' kill him, I face a problem. I'd like to clear up our past misunderstandings, but John Burgess is beyond reasoning.' Estela paused, before saying, 'But I'm sure you know all about Burgess. You must see him at the club, and I know that Yen worked at his travel agency.'

Theresa only nodded.

The travel agents was new, something Burgess had never dabbled with in the past. Now she was past her jet-lag, Estela realised that this slight shift in his business empire must be significant. Burgess took everything he did seriously so she would have to look into it. She began by saying that it was difficult to imagine Yen working for a living. 'He can't have earned very much, the way he would steal from everybody.'

Theresa said it was just his mild klepto streak. It was one way of putting it, like Burger King's passing interest in beef or Héctor Barranco Garza's flirtation with pharmaceuticals. Theresa insisted that Yen was sorted at the travel agents. Mostly because he could get cheap flights to Ibiza and Amsterdam, which is all he ever wanted out of life.

'Last night, I heard you tell Junk that Yen was dealing, but it's not true. Yen would have got the sack if he'd ever been busted. He said that Burgess was paranoid about drugs – because he was once such a criminal and he's now trying to live it down.'

Estela said, 'I only just met Yen, but I don' believe he could be so diligent, keeping his job by keeping his boss sweet.'

Theresa put her half empty cup of tea on the floor. Estela had forgotten to stir it, or bring teaspoons. A thick granular syrup oozed about the bottom of the cup. It was God's truth, Yen never dealt drugs: 'Nearly, everyone deals a little. Or what the cops call dealing, buying more than they need and selling the extra on to a friend as a favour – but Yen didn't even do that. He was always at the bottom of the food chain. Which only made him all the more keen to rush off to Amsterdam every possible weekend. If you don't believe me, ask his friends. Half of them work for Burgess, too. They'll tell you the same thing.'

'I've met some of his friends.'

'There are two called Cozy and Tom, another boy called Jules.'

Estela nodded, Cozy and Tom she knew. She believed Jules was the one who claimed to be the reincarnation of a Dutch sailor. Could Burgess really only employ idiots, drug-hobbyists, the emotionally disturbed?

Estela said, 'Every travel agents I've ever seen, they employ young girls and dress them in air hostess drag. But I suppose Burgess still prefers boys.'

'Burgess isn't gay, is he?'

'The worst kind,' said Estela. 'Like an American novelist, the kind that has to maintain one hundred per cent hetero integrity.'

'What do you mean?'

Estela admitted that she did not know: 'I never could work out what went on under the skin of John Burgess. I thought it was better that I did not try to find out. And I've known him for nearly twenty years.'

'Since the time when he was Manchester's biggest gangster?'

Estela nodded.

'And what were you, his Moll?'

'No.'

Estela must have let a half-beat slip because Theresa said, 'But he was soft on you?'

Estela let that hang; she remembered that St Paul had cursed softness ahead of theft and extortion. Instead, she picked up the cups and saucers and took them through to the kitchen where the radio was playing a wayward version of 'Right On Time'. The news came on just as she finished stacking the plates in the sink. It led with Yen's death, and the news that the Gravity would not reopen until further notice.

Theresa was sat upright, listening, but that was the end of the item. The newscaster moved on to a piece about an attack on an Indian restaurant in Rusholme. The police believed that automatic weapons were involved and were appealing for witnesses.

Theresa said, 'Is that it?'

'What did you expect, a minute's silence?'

Estela regretted her tone immediately she saw Theresa's eyes. Soft tears were collecting against her lashes. Estela knew that she was growing too hard. She needed her pills back. She had to ask – 'Yen stole some tablets from my handbag. Do you know what happened to them?'

Theresa reached under a settee cushion and pulled out a bottle.

'Yen had these with him in the club. I went back for them after he died. I thought it was better the cops didn't find them.'

Theresa took the bottle of Chicadol gratefully, her eyes cast heavenwards in thanks. Opening the child-proof cap, she could not believe how few were left.

'He has taken all these?'

'I guess so. I mean, there was no way I was going to have any. Whatever's gone, he must have taken. Are they dangerous?'

'Not to Yen. Not in his state. But the police surgeon might have a surprise.'

Estela wondered how she could replace the bottle. If she could not persuade anyone to write a fresh prescription, she could hold up a pharmacist. She would have to find a new gun, first.

ELEVEN

Junk was beginning to think his tactics had been off. Burgess was determined to get hold of Theresa. Calling Bernard over on the in-house phone, he only pretended to cover the mouthpiece every time he bawled a new obscenity at Junk. Worse than plain insults, there were threats. Burgess said that if the girl was not bound and delivered sharpish then Junk was going to be looking at the bottom of the Rochdale Canal. Bernard would be on hand to make sure Junk didn't think about swimming.

'When you find her, bring her to the office – no, forget that, the cops might still be over at the club. Wait for me upstairs at the WARP.'

Junk left in Bernard's Lexus, wondering how he was going to avoid finding Theresa. Bernard's solid stream of chat didn't help him think, bludgeoning him and drowning out the Otis Redding CD from the Lexus's trunk-mounted stereo. Otis worried he'd been loving too long. Bernard worried about City's chances of stuffing Arsenal that afternoon. Junk hadn't even known City were playing Arsenal.

'You should be ashamed, John Quay, how do you think City are going to do if we don't get behind them – we're the old school; if we don't show we're loyal, who the fuck is?'

Junk looked out through the windscreen, his eyes strictly forward. He had thrown off past loyalties just as he'd thrown off the evil come-downs between his speed binges. He was still around (where else would he go?), but he didn't have two good eyes any more and if he ever caught sight of his reflection he was glad he didn't see that same face staring back at him, a half-crazed ghost from the rough end of the seventies.

Bernard said, 'Remember how we met, at a game?'

It was an away match: West Ham.

'Those Cockney cunts chasing me all over the fucking show. I ducked behind a garden wall and there you were. John Quay. Trying to dig yourself a hole under the herbaceous border.'

Junk remembered. Bernard had worn an outgrown suede head and a stripey Jackson 5 style tanktop but no shirt. White flab put the knit under stress.

'Arse up, eh, John Quay? Run to ground in the fucking shrubbery. It looked like we were goners. Then Crossy and his lads came around the corner, full pelt. The fucking cavalry, the charge of the fucking black brigade. They saw what was happening and laid those bastards out. We jumped up and started giving it to them as well. Like they say: the victory was ours.'

Bernard was nodding happily; his huge fat head bounced up and down.

'I tell you,' he said. 'That Michael Cross could really fight, the black bastard. He and his boys made good bouncers, so long as they kept off the fucking spliff. Those were the fucking days, eh? Is Crossy still in prison?'

Junk said, 'No. He's out, he's living on Moss Side.'

'I tell you, black football hooligans, it could only happen in Manchester, that's all I can say. They fucking scared me, the way they laid into those Cockneys, and we were on the same side.'

Junk wanted to put a brake on the nostalgia. He said, 'We were on the same side then.'

Bernard sucked on his teeth, an obscene squelch broke over his lips. 'Well, yeah, of course. It was all right having a bunch of black hooligans hanging around in the early days, but when me and Burgess got serious we needed a team with more discipline.'

'Men who'd take orders.'

'Yeah, I don't mind admitting it. Loyalty is important. Those black bastards only ever listened to Crossy.'

Otis Redding was sitting on the dock of the bay. Bernard let him have a moment's peace, before he said what was on his mind: 'What did Michael Cross get, three years?'

'He served two, he got out last year.' said Junk.

'He was lucky.'

'I don't think he saw it that way.'

'Fuck that. He was lucky. He was getting too old to be a hooligan, and he was better off in prison than on the streets. When his boys got busted on that extortion deal, every last one of them got a ten stretch. With Cross already inside, he got away with it. You say he's out now but the rest of them won't be out for seven years. Six years, easy.'

'About that, I reckon.'

'You sure Cross is out? I can't say I've seen him around.'

'He's banned from City for life. And where else would you see him? You stick close to the Gravity, if you're not at home in Knutsford. Michael Cross stays on Moss Side.' Junk wasn't sure whether to risk saying what was on his mind. He decided to say it anyway: 'Why are you asking? Are you afraid of meeting up with him again?'

Bernard looked at him sharply: 'What are you saying?'

'You know what I'm saying.'

'It was just business. Cross and his boys got plenty of work elsewhere. At one point, they must have been doing the security at every other club in town, so why should they care about being cut out of the Gravity? They wouldn't have been interested anyway – not once we'd decided the place was going to be clean. What those black bastards wanted, was clubs with more angles, more business opportunities.'

'There was more to it than that.'

'Yeah,' admitted Bernard. 'A bit more. But, it was down to that half-caste puff. I tell you, he was nothing but fucking trouble.'

'Paul Sorel wasn't half-caste. His mother was.' Junk was thinking how the skinny boy with a natural tan had filled out over the past fifteen years.

'Same difference. That puff caused so much fucking aggravation. I don't know how much you know about it, but he got away with thousands.'

Junk said, 'I know about it.'

He tried to sound confident. At least, he knew some things: some of it rumours, some of it he may have imagined. It was the year his psychoses were officially diagnosed and catalogued, so he guessed he was an unreliable observer. He had black holes large enough to drive a lorry through, he had lapses that could be colonised, coloured red and labelled The People's Republic of China. But this wasn't something he'd blanked on. It was Burgess who had pulled down the screens.

Whatever happened between Burgess and Paul/Estela, they were the only two who knew for sure. Burgess wasn't telling and Paul/Estela had vanished, along with a fortune taken straight from Burgess's private pension fund.

Perhaps five times over the past dozen years, certainly no more than that, Junk and Bernard had edged up to the subject – freaked by nerves, rattled, bottled, goosed and spooked. They had never compared notes, Bernard had always pulled back. The official story, the story with the Burgess stamp, said she had stolen it.

Michael Cross said she hadn't: it was money due, it was her compensation.

Bernard's body moved inside his Crombie great-coat. It might have been a shrug. Whatever it was, Bernard wasn't going to open up. 'Fuck the lot them. Paul Sorel, Michael Cross, every fucking last one of them. I tell you, we were best rid of them. It was better to start the new club with a fresh team.'

'With you in control.'

'Yeah,' said Bernard. 'You got a problem with that, John Quay?'

Bernard would know that Junk wouldn't say either way – whether he had a problem or not. All Junk thought was that Michael Cross and his boys would never have broken into his flat, as Bernard's had done. At least, Michael Cross wouldn't have done it unless he had wanted to, for his own reasons. And if Michael claimed that Burgess's money was taken in lieu of damages, weighed against some kind of rank atrocity, then Junk believed him. Why would he lie? It was Michael who lost out, telling a story like that against Burgess.

Junk sat back in his seat. What would Bernard say if he could see Paul now? With the suave clothes, make-up, tit job; all of it paid for indirectly by Burgess. Junk could hear Bernard brag – that Paul, I had him once, he were all right.

Junk smiled. There was one way to start trouble, he thought. Whether it would help was debatable but he had no way of keeping Theresa from Burgess. He could wind Bernard up. If Bernard got so mad he beat him senseless, it would at least save him from having to hunt Theresa down.

'You know what I reckon?' said Junk. 'Burgess was more sorry to lose Paul than he was sorry to lose the money.'

Bernard turned from the wheel and glared at Junk.

'That's a fucking lie.'

'What do you think? Have you seen with him anyone – any women?'

'Fuck off, John Quay. He's just one of those that's not interested, not everyone is interested in sex. What about you, for a start? Are you a puff? I haven't seen you shagging anything either.'

'If it comes to that, I've never seen you shagging anyone. But like I always thought, big lad, it's just talk with you, isn't it? What I reckon is, you and Burgess have an understanding. Burgess slips you a length of spam javelin and you fucking love it. I bet you call your boys around to watch Uncle Bernard taking it up the shitter.'

Bernard slammed on the brakes, a man gone apoplectic at the wheel. He grabbed Junk with his left arm and pulled him across to the driver's seat. Junk felt his spine was going to crack, he was so twisted inside his seatbelt. Bernard had hauled him halfway across the car, turning him around so his face was inches from Bernard's own. He could see the shower of scars across Bernard's nose, the deeper scar running across his eyebrow where someone had onced smashed a bottle into razor-sharp splinters. He could see the black lines across the top of Bernard's front teeth, at the point the false crowns met the gum. But he couldn't hear what Bernard was saying as Bernard squeezed the blood out of his neck. It seemed to Junk that Bernard had managed to turn his neck all the way around. He felt like the cat in a Tom and Jerry cartoon, when Tom's body is cork-screwed by the untalking dog. Bernard forced Junk head-first into the steering wheel, between the spokes and the rim. He began trying to turn the wheel with Junk's head inside. Junk heard Otis singing 'Try A Little Tenderness' and all he could think was: this is ridiculous. It hurt less than being strangled – Junk believed that he could cope with this, and Bernard surely couldn't think of a way of topping it.

Forcing someone's head into a Lexus steering wheel had to be a dead-end.

'Take me around to that girl's house, now.'

Bernard had run out of steam. He pulled Junk's head out of the wheel and threw him back on to the passenger seat.

'And don't fuck around, you fucking fucked-up fucking fuck-wit.'

Junk gave in. He was still conscious, so what else could he do? They were already at the foot of Kingsway. Junk told Bernard to take the next right. Inside two minutes, they were parked outside a row of terraced houses. Theresa's home stood in the middle.

'That's it?' asked Bernard.

Junk nodded: 'Let's go.'

Bernard swung his fat legs out of his door and took four shoulder-swinging strides to Theresa's front door. Junk kept behind him, pointing him right. 'She's called O'Donnell.'

Bernard started banging on the door, hammering with the edge of his curled fist. Junk was thinking, Jesus, he could take the whole door down if he's not careful. Bernard shouted 'O'Donnell, O'Donnell', as he smashed away at the door. There was no sound from inside. After thirty seconds, Bernard stooped to peer through the letterbox. Sitting back on huge haunches, his heavy chest pressed up against the door, his stubby fingers poked through the narrow slit and flicked at the inside flap of the letterbox. It didn't look as though Bernard had seen any sign of life, but he continued to shout.

'O'Donnell.'

Nothing. Bernard quit for a second.

'What's her Christian name?' he asked, looking over to Junk.

'Theresa.'

Bernard stuck his fingers back through the letterbox: 'Theresa O'Donnell, open this door now.'

There was still nothing.

Bernard straightened: 'You try.'

Junk stepped to the door and started hammering, yelling in the deepest voice he could register: 'Miss O'Donnell, we know you're in there.'

A fat hand grabbed hold of his pony tail. Junk heard Bernard say 'Shit, you bastard' before his head smashed against the door, his forehead cracking against the iron letterbox. As he bounced and crumpled to the pavement, his nose welled up and burst with fresh blood.

From street-level, Junk saw Bernard's feet pounding away up the street to the ginnell and the narrow passage-way that led to the back of the terraces. In half a minute, he heard screams. Bernard came crashing back through the passage pulling Theresa by her arm. Theresa tried to slow him down, digging her heels into the paving slabs but Bernard hardly broke his stride as he pulled her to his car. Taking her to the driver's side, he opened the door with one hand and threw her across the front seats.

The last Junk saw of them, lifting his smashed nose up off the pavement, was Bernard bundling Theresa's legs up and following her into the car. Theresa was still upside down as the Lexus pulled away from the kerb. Junk thought that he could probably get to his feet, but why bother? He had fucked up, it was better to stay as he was.

Theresa's front door opened. Estela reached the edge of the pavement in time to see the Lexus disappear around the block opposite.

'Nice one, Junk,' she said. 'You brought Bernard right to the door.'

Junk said, 'I thought Theresa would think it was the bailiffs, come to get her poll tax arrears. I thought she would just run out the back. No one uses the front door.'

'I recognised Bernard's voice anyway. I was ahead of Theresa, through her back gate, when a fist came from nowhere and cracked me on the ear. When Bernard grabbed Theresa, I was still lying in the yard, wondering what had hit me.'

'Bernard didn't recognise you?' asked Junk.

'No,' said Estela. 'If he had done, he would not have dared lay a hand on me. The next time I meet him though, he'll know. It is going to be the last thing he ever knows, believe me.'

TWELVE

'So Burgess has kidnapped Theresa. What does he really have on her? You say he has no pictures of her actually pulling the trigger.'

Junk said: 'He could hurt her. Bernard could kill her, or worse. I'm responsible, I told Burgess that she could link him with Yen's death.'

Junk explained how his reasoning had worked, when he made up the huge story about Yen being a drug dealer and convinced Burgess that his death would lead to greater trouble.

'I was winging it. Trying to think of a way to keep her out of the hands of the cops. I told Burgess that I bought all of his own cocaine off Yen.'

'She has nothing to worry about, believe me.' Estela smoothly, soothingly, poured out the tea. She had managed to persuade Junk to get off the pavement and come into the house.

Junk wasn't listening: 'Bernard's taken Theresa to the bar. If I get over there – I could be there before Burgess arrives.'

Estela said, 'Leave it. You have other things to do. I need a gun – you have to help me get one.'

'What do I know about guns?'

'You used to know something about guns. I remember you waving a pistol in a club once, screaming that you were going to blow everyone away if they don' switch off the music and leave your head alone.'

'I don't remember that.'

'It was during your blue period.'

'What would I be doing with a gun? If I'd had one in those days, I would have shot myself – not anyone else.'

'Maybe you have a stronger life-instinct than you think. You came through the seventies just fine. I have to say, I was surprised to see you. I thought you would be dead for certain.'

'Sometimes I can't believe I'm still alive. Then I catch sight of myself – I'm not alive. This is someone different.'

'When you talk like that, the more I begin to think you've lost the plot. I once read that incidences of schizophrenia are highest amongst young urban black males. You are neither black nor young – statistically you are not due for another schizo-episode. But if you are, you can wait until I find a gun.'

'Are you schizo?' asked Junk.

Estela looked aghast: 'No.'

'That's good. I was only asking, anyway,' said Junk. He drank his tea, and after a while began to think: 'You don't need me to get you a gun. Michael Cross is still living on Moss Side. If I give you the address – you can go see him and I'll find Theresa.'

'Michael Cross. I thought he'd spend his whole life in prison if he don' leave Manchester.'

'He's been inside, now he's out. Everyone else in his crew is still banged up.'

Estela took on a wistful look. It seemed to Junk, everyone was getting on a nostalgia trip. She said, 'I'd like to see Michael. Okay, phone me a taxi – I'll let you go after Theresa.'

Amjad took the call from his uncle. He had been sitting at the back of the radio room for an hour – and every single person who stopped by had asked him what he thought about the windows being blown out of Jabhar's restaurant. He'd been on the shift, then, and the night had been dead; he'd not had a call for over an hour. That's how come he saw the car pull up opposite his uncle's cab company in Rusholme, right outside Jab's curry house. Two black lads jumped out of the car and started shooting. Amjad remembered one having trouble with his gun. Before he managed to get a good grip on it with both hands, he was spraying bullets in all directions. His gun arm jerking up and down, his body shaking like a spastic rattling an electric fence. Still, they managed to shoot out the windows at Jab's and totally wrecked the inside.

Amjad went over later and had a look at the damage. By then the cops were picking through the debris and asking for witnesses. They didn't find a single one. Amjad played dumb to the police but that didn't work on the other drivers, his uncle's family or his little brother and all of his idiot friends.

What did Amjad reckon? He was fucked if he knew, that's what he said when anyone asked. He just repeated for the hundredth time what he'd seen. Most of the other drivers, his uncle too, were wondering if they'd get drawn into any trouble. No one fancied messing around with machine guns. It's not a war, said Amjad. There's no reason to go thinking that the cab company will get shot up. His younger brother was the one who thought they should get serious; they should show that they weren't going to get fucked over by anyone. If the gangs over on Moss Side are packing Uzis, then they'd get Uzis too. There were a lot more fucking guns in Karachi than any of the blacks could get off their Yardie heroes, no matter how much they were ready to pay. Amjad slapped his little brother over the head, 'Who said they'd got Uzis? I was the only one who saw anything. You live in a fucking dream, you dick.'

Everyone knew that Jab's windows had been blown out

because Jab's uncle was hiking up the price of heroin. Amjad wasn't going to get drawn into any drug gang stuff. As far as he knew, Jab wasn't involved either. Just because Jab's uncle ate at his curry house, now and again, Jab's whole investment goes up in gunfire. And dickheads like Amjad's little brother wanted to get involved. He was glad to take the call and get out of the shop.

Amjad pulled up outside a terrace in Levenshulme and sounded his horn. He was adjusting his rearview mirror when he saw the skinny white man come out of an alley, further up the terrace. Amjad knew the man, recognised his squint and the scrawny pony tail at the back of his head. A real skinny cunt; Amjad reckoned he'd got that way from sampling too many of the drugs he was dealing. He had a druggy name. Amjad couldn't remember it, but he never remembered any of those stupid street names. His little brother wanted everyone to call him something dumb – something with numbers in it instead of words, like six-pack or seven-up.

The black gangster who'd shot up Jab's place had a really stupid name: The Tasmanian. That was close enough. Amjad never forgot a face, but had difficulty with any name that didn't mean something. Or worse, a name that meant something, but only something stupid. Amjad knew of kids who were calling themselves after stuff in the supermarket: Radion Automatic, Pepsi, Vimto. The Tasmanian was named after a cartoon character, Amjad remembered that. It wasn't such an inappropriate name. The way he'd stood outside Jab's restaurant, spraying a ton of bullets into the place, he probably thought he was in a cartoon.

Amjad watched the skinny man edge around a couple of cars and pass by the taxi without looking. Amjad noticed everything; this man only seemed to see one thing at a time. The way he stared, he had a habit of concentrating on one little spot at a time. Then he would jump or twitch as he noticed the next little spot right beside it. That might come from the drugs or from having only one eye. The last time Amjad had seen him he was with the Tasmanian, stood outside the Moss Side gym, buying or selling something wrapped up in a package. When the Tasmanian poked a hole in the package with a knife and tasted whatever stuck to the tip, Amjad knew it was a powder. When the Tasmanian offered his knife over, the skinny man had refused. Maybe he wasn't on drugs any more but he must have gone through a ton of the stuff to have ended up such a mess.

Two minutes later, the woman poked her head out of the same alley. She stopped short of the pavement, keeping under the shelter of the two terraces. It was raining and she wanted to make sure the taxi was there before she risked wetting her hair. The last time Amjad saw her, she'd been wearing a scarf. He sounded his horn, she stepped over briskly in her high heels. As she got into the back of the cab, she gave an address off the Alexandra Park Estate.

Two nights back, he'd not been able to work out what she was. He'd not believed that she was American. Now he wondered if she was black. She was definitely the same woman, whatever. And the boy she'd had with her, he was definitely the one whose picture was on the front page of the *Manchester Evening News* – an italicised blurb gave out that he was dead.

Amjad didn't know whether to let on. If she was a friend of that skinny man, maybe she also knew the motherfucker who shot up Jab's restaurant. If he was tactful, maybe he'd learn something. It was a habit, collecting information, but it was rarely useful. Anyway, he'd had a bellyful of trouble for one night. With Jab's restaurant and this boy's death both happening on the same night, the whole Gunchester thing would be blown up again. The town would be swarming with television people and journalists, like it was a few months back. He decided to keep quiet.

Taking the route through the estate in Fallowfield, he passed close by City's stadium. The unlit floodlights scratched at the rain-heavy clouds out of boredom. Amjad pulled another rear-mirror look at the woman. She was certainly something. He decided he would say something after all.

'You're American, aren't you? Where you from?'

It was pretty safe. She didn't sound American, but what would he know. He had a cousin in New York and he knew there were all kinds of Americans. Maybe he should go over and visit the family, although his cousin was a fourth cousin, now he came to think about it.

'South America. My mother came from Surinam,' said Estela. Odd, she had told the cabbie the truth. It felt as though she was picking up an old conversation.

Amjad said, 'Sorry, love, I've never heard of it. Is that where you live?'

'I travel around quite a bit.' Estela realised why he looked familiar. She had been so out of it the other night, but that was certainly when she had seen him. She had him placed and, catching his eyes in the Nissan's mirror, he had her, too. She told him to pull over: now.

Amjad pulled on to the kerb. Estela asked his name.

'Why do you want to know?'

'Why don' you want to tell me?'

Amjad reached over to the passenger seat, underneath his jacket.

'Don' move.' Estela's voice had turned hard.

'I was just getting the paper,' said Amjad. What was this? It was more like a film than real life. Did everyone have guns on their minds? Amjad took the newspaper from off the passenger seat and handed it over to Estela. She could see the front page for herself: 'Double-Barrelled, Two Gun Battles in One Night'. The page was split in half down the centre: Yen's photograph was on the left, a near-demolished shopfront was pictured on the right.

'Nice photograph; what does it say underneath?' asked Estela.

'Can't you read English?'

'I can read. I wanted to know if you had read it.'

'I've not had chance,' said Amjad. 'To tell the truth, I were more bothered about the other story. I know the owner of the restaurant.'

Estela could see that it used to be a restaurant, if she looked hard enough at the creased picture. She skipped over the curry house story to read that the only witnesses to Yen's death were a DJ employed at the Gravity and a Brazilian tourist. What was this rubbish? She was not a witness. She had been a passer-by, that was all. She should sue. She tossed the paper back to Amjad.

'Poor boy,' she said. Amjad nodded.

After a moment's silence, Amjad relented. He introduced himself, Estela held out her hand and they shook. 'Estela. Hello.'

'What are you doing in Moss Side?' asked Amjad.

'I have to look someone up.'

'Who?'

Estela was not sure whether she should say. She had an address, although Junk had not been too specific. He had given her the name of a block and told her to ask around. She envisioned an afternoon trailing around cafés, pool halls, gyms, she didn't know how many other places. She might have to spend all afternoon with this cabbie – unless she decided to walk. She could at least tell Amjad who he was supposed to be looking for. There was a time when everyone knew who Michael Cross was. She told him.

'Michael Cross,' Amjad repeated. 'What do you want to see him for?'

'It's personal,' said Estela. Then felt stupid, it only made the whole thing seem stranger – the beautifully presented tourist hunting Moss Side for an ageing gangsta. She tried to turn the interrogation around. 'What do you know about Michael Cross?'

'He used to run a gang called the Western Union. But that was years ago – before this kind of stuff . . .'

Amjad prodded at the *Manchester Evening News*, pointing at the trashed shopfront, Jabhar's curry house.

'. . . But they all ended up in prison. Michael Cross was sent down first, after he was caught fighting at a soccer match. Once he was inside, the Western Union started losing their contracts. They worked security all over town but the club owners were under pressure not to use them.'

'Who from?'

Amjad shrugged. 'Pressure. Who knows? Anyone who's got a stake in the town's nightlife. The problem was, no one in Manchester dared take a contract away from the Western Union. So what the club owners did, they brought in a security firm from Liverpool. They reckoned that coming from so far away, they wouldn't be scared of Crossy's boys. It worked, for a while.

'No one in the Western Union gang knew where these new bouncers lived. They couldn't go round their homes and threaten them. But with Michael Cross inside, they reckoned they were losing face if they didn't hit back hard. So, what they do, they took it to the clubs. One place, they had this man on the floor, making him suck off the barrel of a gun. They smashed half his teeth in.

Another place, they kick in the firedoors at the back and walk straight through the dancers and everything, firing guns into the ceiling. They wanted to show that they had the bottle to go anywhere.

'All that happened, seven clubs had to close before the police did anything. When the police got them, finally, they wound up with ten years a piece.'

'But not Michael Cross?'

'No. He's out. He still lives in Moss Side but doesn't run gangs any more. I heard he hangs out at the Croner Hotel.'

'How do you know that?' Estela didn't think that the times had changed so much. Some of the Pakis might have broken with the Koran enough to go drinking, but she couldn't believe that they hung out in Alexandra Park at the Croner Hotel.

'I work sixteen hours a day, driving around South Manchester. I end up knowing these things.'

Estela thought it sounded odd. If Michael Cross spent all day in the Croner Hotel – he must be selling dope or something. What else could he do? She guessed that's why Amjad knew him. All she said was: 'We'll try there, then.'

THIRTEEN

Amjad stopped outside the Croner Hotel and told Estela she was sure to find Michael Cross inside. Estela asked him to wait. If Michael was there, she'd be right out to pay him. 'No offence,' he said, 'I trust you.' But he wasn't hanging around. Not today, not when things had got so heavy recently. Amjad told her: 'Dead cert, Michael Cross would be there, no worries.' Estela stayed in the back of Amjad's Nissan for a while to watch the boys in pin-rolls and puffa jackets cruise up and down the road on their mountain bikes. Every time one passed the cab, he would look down – half-interested because his job depended upon him remaining aware. Otherwise, every one of them looked indifferent. They pushed their pedals around in long slow movements, standing up from their seats and scanning the streets in equally long and slow circular movements. They looked like some kind of super-evolved bird that had given up its wings for the bicycle. Black herons with their heads cocked against the breeze.

Estela paid and thanked Amjad – see you around – and entered through the side door, the entrance that Amjad had pointed out for her. Sweet clouds of dope hung frozen under the pool table lights. Waiting until her eyes grew acclimatised to the heavy fug, Estela stepped out.

It did not take her long to find Michael Cross. He was stood by one of the two pool tables in the shadows to the rear of the Croner Hotel. Running around the three walls of the pool area was a shelf built to hold the players' drinks. Michael was leaning against it, at ease, his elbows braced against the shelf-edge and his feet slightly apart on the floor. Estela wasn't fooled. She saw a body that could straighten and sprint in a moment. He had kept himself in shape over the past years. A different shape to her, he was barely changed. Maybe a few more lines, enough to prove age carries experience. The dreads were new, but Michael Cross had always been wise to fashions. The short, un-rasta locks were woven flat to the top of the crown until they burst out like a comet tail behind his head – as though he were locked in a cartoonish hyper-drive. In motion, even when he was sagging against a pool room wall.

Walking towards him, a white boy cut across her path and reached Michael first. She heard the boy ask for an eighth. Michael reached under the shelf and came up with a knife that must have been stuck blade-first into the shelf's underside. Taking a black stick of resin from his pocket, he cut a sliver from one end and pushed it towards the boy with a wink. Michael pocketed the note and few coins the boy offered, nodding thanks as the boy shuffled away. It was only then he saw Estela. She could have laughed, he was so intent on cool seduction.

'Where're you going to, honey, because I tell you, I want to come along for the ride.'

Michael Cross had a lazy grin, breaking open on to a band of white between his full purple lips. Like an orthodonist's dream, framed by tear-drop dimples.

'You look sweet, I mean it. You could light up this room like you're a thousand-watt bulb. Just let me supply the candle-power.'

'I don' think so, Michael,' Estela said. 'You far too old for me.'

His eyes, that had shone like pools of limpid Bovril, narrowed. His smile began to chew at itself. Estela enjoyed the pause. Beneath the surface, Michael thrashed about for a clue. Estela admired the outward calm. He could not place her.

'Do I know you? Because if I'd had the pleasure, I would have bet on me remembering,' Michael said, finally.

'Estela Santos.'

Michael flexed effortlessly, and stood upright to meet her outstretched hand. His grip was dry.

'I wish I knew who you were, sister.'

'You know me, Michael,' Estela lisped sweetly before dropping her voice to a nasal drone. 'I don't believe you won't let on to me, you twat.'

It took a second to register: 'Paul! What've they fucking done to you?'

Now they were sitting in the other bar, drinking together in the near-empty calm of the spacious lounge area, they had a chance to catch up. Estela had said she was working for some businessmen, over in the States. Michael nodded, Yeah? He was doing this and that: you know, keeping up appearances. There was still one thing bothering him, Estela could tell.

'Are you going to lose that voice?' he had to ask.

'Does it upset you?'

'It doesn't do anything for me, that's for sure.'

'It will grow on you,' said Estela in melodic Anglo-Latin. She loved the way a burst of her Manchester accent had shocked Michael out of his cool, she could swear she saw smoke blowing out of his ears.

'I hear all the old boys are in prison,' she said.

Michael had reasserted his kharmic deportment. Estela always admired his balance. His voice purred with the mellifluence of a power-tool, turned-on but not put to work – only stirring the air.

'That's right, the Western Union is out of business. The brothers got heavy-duty sentences. By the time they're out we'll all be too old for that kind of shit. I'm sweet. I tell you, I walk through the estate, and all these kids come up saying I'm the OG – the godfather. But I'm through with anything but dealing a little draw. I'm taking it easy. I'll be playing dominoes and drinking rum before long.'

'You were sent down, too. It's what I heard,' Estela said. Michael let his arms hang by his side: Yeah. Shrugging; it was a stupid business.

'I still can't fucking believe that. I got sent down for being a football hooligan. And that was in, like, 1988.'

'You don' think you were too mature for that kind of thing?'

'Too right. I hadn't been on that tip for years. At the time, there was all kind of things in the papers about cracking down on the Waving Tide Of Hooliganism, if you believe the papers. The same time, the clubs are pledging to get heavy with the Small Violent Minority and the government are threatening a whole load of new shit. I didn't pay attention to the hype, it's not like I was going to get into anything. I was going to watch a match, that was it.

'City were playing Everton. Even before kick-off, there's chanting from the other side about the niggers on the pitch and the niggers on the terraces. But when it's at a match, you don't notice it any more. It just goes on all the time, you drown them out by singing louder.

'What I didn't realise, because I wasn't even looking for it, was the coppers keeping an eye on me. Maybe they thought that if City were playing stone-cold racists like half the people following Everton, then it's going to be a brother who starts any trouble.'

Michael paused. Estela sensed a pulse of anger, beginning to break beneath Michael's composed front.

'After we left the ground, the police keep us separate from the Everton crowd. We can see all these kids from

Everton flicking V's and shouting Nigger. We just face them down. Then someone breaks through the line of police – not even a black lad. There's a surge forward, we clout a few kids as we're pushed past them. That's it. The next day, I see myself on the front page of the *Manchester Evening News* – Hard Core Hooligan. I've been filmed by a video camera in the ground, just chanting on the terraces. They got me at the right moment, I look like an animal ready to tear some cunt apart – but I know I was only singing. The police swear that I was the one who orchestrated the trouble after the match.

'The police give evidence that I've been behind most of the violence at Maine Road for the past fifteen years. They say I'm known on the Kippax as the Black Napoleon. All other kinds of shit, you know. That it was time to make an example of people like me. In the end, I couldn't believe they only gave me three years. I thought they were going to roast my nuts and hang them over the ground.'

'That's too bad.'

'Too right.'

'I hated prison,' Estela admitted. 'That's why you had to get me out.'

A nod, Yeah, he'd helped her out. 'But with me, I couldn't believe I stayed out for so long so I just rolled over and accepted it. If you're a face, you know, you think that you'll get banged up eventually. But serving two years . . .' Michael shrugged again, in a way that Estela read as: two wasted years.

'And even then I could say I was lucky because I spent some of it in Strangeways. At least I was in Manchester, living in the same city as my family. But after the Strangeways riot, the Home Office ended up transferring me to Scotland.'

Estela picked up on Michael's mention of his family. 'You've got a couple of boys haven't you?'

'No. Now I got four sons, two daughters – from three different women. I'm married to one of them. I don't know.' Michael shrugged again. This time Estela couldn't read it.

'They're all local. I could open my wallet, I'd show you photographs – of the kids as babies, school pictures, and they're all beautiful. But now my sons are gangstas. Like I said, I'm sweet. But if they don't end up doing serious time, then they'll end up dead, shot on the street by another boy with a gun and a mountain bike.'

Estela could read the shrug now.

She said, 'I was hoping you liked guns, because I really need one. But if you can't help with that, I'd appreciate a place to stay. I have a feeling that the police are squatting outside my place.'

Michael's mouth seemed a little tight: you're bringing trouble down on my head? But he didn't say anything. Instead, he stood and walked to the bar which stood in the centre of the pub.

The two halves of the Croner were closed to each other. Only the bar opened on to both the pool room and the lounge. When Michael reached the wooden counter, he leant over and beckoned to someone out of sight in the back half of the pub. He held up a finger for Estela: just one second.

After a moment, a younger man joined Michael at the bar. Michael took something – it could only be the stick of resin – from his pocket and handed it over. They shook briefly, sliding their palms across each other's hands until only their fingertips touched: yeah, see you. Michael returned to Estela.

'Clive can take care of business. We'll step over to my place. I should tell you to fuck off, but I always feel responsible for anyone I've broke out of prison. I'll give you a smoke, some decent shit I've got. We can talk.'

FOURTEEN

'How long have they been here?'

'About fifteen minutes.'

Junk peered around Billy the Bouncer and looked down the length of the WARP. The cops were stood in two groups, one by the bar and one further towards the back of the long room. There were five in all, every one in plain clothes. They might as well have walked in with sandwich boards over their shoulders warning you that anything you might say would be taken down and used as evidence.

'What do they want?'

Billy didn't know.

Once Junk stepped out of the shadow of Billy's big shoulders he found out. They wanted a word with him. Before they saw him, they were stood making theatrically inconsequential small talk. When Junk walked into the room they stopped and looked straight at him. Junk thought, oh shit. He darted to the top end of the bar and stooped under the trap. The cops weren't sure what to do – they had the exits covered and couldn't decide whether to follow Junk under the counter. Two of them hurried down to the far end of the bar, keeping pace with Junk as he trotted along on the other side of the counter.

'John Quay,' they shouted, over the heads of the people waiting to be served.

Junk nodded at them in the gaps between the bartenders and lunchtime drinkers: 'Sorry, I'm in a bit of a hurry.'

'Mr Quay, can we have a word with you?'

'Not today, lads,' said Junk.

At the top of the bar, a policeman and woman dropped under the counter and gave chase. After disentangling themselves from the boy at the capuccino machine, they fought their way between the bartenders and tried to catch Junk.

Junk had already disappeared through a side door. He started to climb the stairs to the rooms above. If he found Bernard and Theresa quickly, the police would catch him there. At least the cops would see Theresa with Bernard. If anything should happen to her, Bernard would head the list of possible suspects. Junk hoped that it would be enough to keep her safe. Burgess could not want more police interest in his affairs. He surely would not harm Theresa, not once Junk had brought a wagonload of policemen to stand witness. He pounded along the upstairs landing and skidded to a halt as he heard Bernard's voice.

'I had a few girls named Theresa one time, they were all right.'

Theresa was sat on a chair by the window, Bernard was leaning back against a wall – looking her over. He turned to greet Junk as the door burst open.

'All right, John Quay. You look a bit flushed.'

'I've been running. Burgess hasn't arrived yet, then?'

'No,' said Bernard. 'Have you come to apologise for being so uncooperative when I came to fetch Theresa here?'

'I took you to the right house, didn't I?' Junk turned to Theresa. 'How are you, Tréz, anyway?'

She gave him a brave smile. She was surprised to see all the police stumble in behind Junk.

'Fucking hell,' said Bernard. 'The boys in blue.'

'Mr John Quay?' The lead officer was sweating lightly under the V-neck of his golfing jumper.

'That's right.' Junk raised the eyebrows above his good

and bad eye in mock surprise. 'Did you want to see me about something?'

The police identified themselves professionally: could he come with them to the station? They wanted to follow up last night's interview with a few questions.

'Do you think I should bring my lawyer with me?' Junk nodded over at Theresa. 'Ms Theresa O'Donnell, of Levenshulme.'

'Is she a lawyer?'

'She's still a student,' said Junk.

'But to be brief, she'll do in an emergency,' said Bernard, at ease against the wall. 'Although I think you'll find she's an art student.'

'Well, she's educated,' shrugged Junk.

'If you feel that you need a lawyer, we can arrange for your own or a duty solicitor to meet you at the station. But we really only want a chat, Mr Quay. I don't believe you'll need representation but it's up to you, of course.' The police were becoming impatient.

'I'll tell Burgess you dropped by, John Quay. I'm sure we can get you a lawyer out of petty cash.'

Estela and Michael made for the door and stepped back on to the street. The figures on mountain bikes still patrolled the area. When Estela passed by any one of them with Michael, they would nod or hold up their hands in salute. Out to their front, the tower blocks rose up as pebble-dashed silos. Michael cut across a bank of grass in sloping strides before realising that Estela was no longer beside him.

'I'm not going down there in these heels,' she said.

'Fucking hell, Paul.'

'Fuck you, nigger. It's Estela.'

Michael broke into a smile and retreated to the pavement: 'We'll take the long way round. I would have helped you down, but I didn't want none of these kids seeing me holding hands with an old slapper like you.'

The stairs up to Michael's flat were as squalid as any she had seen before. The graffiti was in English but was unspeakable; somewhere a psychotic was jotting down passages on half the women who lived in the area. On the third landing, Estela slipped on the burnt and twisted Coca-Cola cans that lay strewn across the cement floor. She recognised them as home-made crack pipes. On the fourth, they stepped on to a walkway where the cold air almost washed away the urine-soaked stairs she had left behind. Michael held out his arm: this way. With the gesture, he sank back into the idea that he was with a woman; as he sometimes did in the past.

Before Michael finished turning the key in his door, it was opened by a young black woman, showing lightly of her pregnancy. The look she gave Estela had teeth. There was no doubt what she thought Estela was. Estela was thinking: mm-mm, Michael's sweet babymother. Michael greeted the girl extravagantly and introduced her as Josette. The girl was part-way down the hall before he could introduce Estela.

They walked through to a room that did not seem unspacious. The bright greenery of the pot plants along the window sill, all legal shrubs, and the batik wall hangings made this front room welcoming. Beyond the window, there was another world.

'Take a seat, Es-Tel-A,' said Michael, taking pleasure in pronouncing the name. 'Let Josette put the kettle on.'

'Let Josette say Go Fuck Yourself.' Josette stood in the door. Now that she had told him where to go, she faced him down.

'Josette, honey.' Michael tried winning her with his smile and dimples.

'What are you doing bringing women here? You think

I'm going to shimmy around bringing you tea and biscuits while you work at this slag in my front room? You'd better think again, you no-good geriatric shithead. What's that I heard the boys calling you? OG. Original Gangsta? Fuck that. Beat-up Old Grandfather.' Josette looked ready to spit on him.

'Josette, honey.'

Estela couldn't keep from laughing: 'You tell him, sister. I got no interest in the black creep, 'cept he mek tea for both of us.'

'You heard the woman, and you know where the kettle is,' said Josette.

Michael looked around from Estela to Josette: 'I don't fucking believe . . .'

'Get in that kitchen. And you make sure you put the milk in a jug before you get back here with our brews.' Josette stood away from the door, giving him the room he needed to slink into the kitchen. Michael took it, disappearing into the kitchen area beyond.

Josette sat opposite Estela, smoothing out her dress as she folded her bare smooth legs.

'Estela,' she said. 'I don't believe I seen you before.'

'I am an old friend of Michael's. But just a friend.'

'You don't need to explain. But I'm going to keep that man on the run. I don't want him slipping if he wants to stay around with me.'

'Are you married?' asked Estela.

'He's got a long way to go before I'll marry him,' Josette said.

Michael returned from the kitchen. He was holding a white plastic jug-kettle in his hand. Set into its side was a calibrated transparent tube. On its inside, a red float. Michael was pointing to the tube, puzzled.

'Josette. What's this? When the little ball moves to the top, that mean the water's boiled?'

'Are you serious?' Josette was staring at him. There was a pause, Michael didn't know whether to answer: he was serious.

'Just fill it with water and switch it on, dickhead.'

When Michael returned to the kitchen, Josette looked over to Estela and shook her head in disbelief: who allowed him to grow so old, so stupid?

Michael did not completely mess up on the tea. While the three waited for it to brew, he began work on a joint. Josette was telling him, 'You don't need to put so much care into that: you won't be smoking it while I'm still in the room.'

'It'll do the baby good, give it a mellow character like its father.'

'Make it stunted, that's all. Have you never heard of passive smoking?'

'That's what smoking is for: passivity, honey.'

Michael had to wait until Josette had drunk her tea and left. She wished Estela all the best and explained she was seeing her mother. That left Estela alone with Michael to talk about the old times and why, in these new times, she wanted to play with guns. Michael admitted that guns made him anxious.

'The Western Union was the first posse to use guns in Manchester. What kind of rep is that, when there's always going to be another psycho who's even keener to shoot it out.'

'I heard already about how the boys were sent down. They had taken to holding up rival posses with shotguns.'

Michael blew on the end of a long, cornet-shaped spliff. Taking a drag and holding the smoke for a six-count, he exhaled and started talking.

'I was out of it at the time. If I hadn't been in prison, maybe I could have worked out a better way of doing things. Some of the boys would visit me inside. As if it wasn't bad enough being locked away from my family, they were telling me how great it was on the outside. They were saying: it's the Summer of Love, man. There were these huge parties, up to ten thousand people in fields and warehouses, playing techno and trance. Everyone was doing ecstasy and acid, getting on one and talking peace and unity. I didn't miss out on the ecstasy, you could get it in prison. But it's not the same, is it? It's not as though I was going to leap on the tables and start dancing. There was dancing the week we broke on to the roof of the prison during the riots. We danced for the TV cameras. But the ecstasy was wasted, it's not as if anyone was going to start one great big love-in in prison. Maybe if you'd been there, some of the guys might have tried to get it on. But otherwise, no chance.

'The Western Union was running raves, or doing the security for other outfits. When they came to visit me, they were saying: what a fucking unbelievable buzz out there. They were telling me that the energy was incredible. I was banged up, so I had time to be cynical. They believed Manchester was on the edge of some great new experience. I thought they'd got religious. They were telling me that even at City, all the casuals were doing acid. At evening matches, they were so busy tripping off on the lights and dancing around, they didn't even notice there was a game on. I watched some of it on telly. The whole of City's end were waving giant inflatable bananas – and with the hoods pulled up on their tops, they looked like a crowd of psychedelic monks: the Brotherhood of The Day-Glo Banana.'

Michael took another long draw.

'I read about some fans travelling over to Europe on the ferries. They had some kind of rave on board, but when they arrived in Ostend, there were three missing. They'd disappeared halfway across the Channel. You never know where you're going to end up on a trip. Acid's a white man's drug, anyway. You don't get brothers trying acid more than once, unless they're already crazy.

'You know what it means to be black. You're scared of insanity. Maybe white men get it too – I wouldn't know, maybe some of them. Half of them are already mad. The reason they're not scared of it – they are mad already. Let them fry on acid, they can relax and enjoy it. But a brother knows what it's like to be terrified of going insane. The one thing you can't let happen is lose your head and let the demons get hold of you. It doesn't matter where a brother's from, he knows.

'A brother can't do acid, he can't touch psychedelics. A brother can't mess with his head because he's already got the fear of insanity etched on the inside of his black skull. If he took a trip, he might believe he's gone insane and end up mad, anyway. And he can't get that knowledge out of his head.'

Now he looked over to Estela: 'Is that what you're trying to do, now that you've switched sex? Are you trying to erase that fear? You thought that if you were a woman you'd be able to wipe out the nightmares. You thought: yeah, a bubble-head, a brainless bimbo. There'll never be any reason to think, you believed you'd be safe.'

'You're getting too personal, Michael.' Estela held her voice steady, while she held firm on Michael's eyes. 'I don' want bad blood between us.'

'You were always an airhead, you hadn't got the fucking brains to recognise the terrors. Now you come back here, and the only thing you want is for me to find you a gun. Is that because you're missing your cock already?'

'I never had any reason to miss my cock,' said Estela. 'And I never thought of any woman as an airhead. Whatever I was, whether I was scared of ending up mad or not, I never believed women were the brainless ones – not like you and your boys.'

'I've learnt differently, now.'

'You learnt differently, because you had to learn. I never had to learn, I knew which direction I was heading in. And one more thing, before we close this business and I forget everything you said,' Estela took a long count, knowing that Michael would not be able to speak no matter the length of her pause, 'the reason I was never scared, I had faith in my destiny.'

'Destiny shit.'

'I'm warning you, Michael. You insult me, but you don' insult my religion.'

'Who are you, Santos Mother Theresa of the Silicone Tits?'

'Yes.' Pause. 'Now pass the Rizlas over and I'll give them my blessing.'

FIFTEEN

Junk stepped out of the squad car on to the hard ridged floor of the underground carpark. Squatting above him were the million stone tons of the Greater Manchester Police Headquarters, Old Trafford. Walking beneath the low ceiling of the causeway, he could feel every gramme of dust in every stone poised over his head. DC Havers shadowed him on his blind side. DS Mayhew tagged him on his right, past neat rows of Peugeot 30-somethings parked nose to the wall, all identical to the car that brought him to Old Trafford.

At the sunlit mouth to the carpark, a crowd of policemen were gathered around a boxy slate grey van, cables spilling out of its open doors and an antenna fixed to its roof.

DS Mayhew said, 'See that. That'll be the BBC.'

DC Havers wanted to know if it was TV or radio. Neither of them knew.

The two detectives had introduced themselves on the drive to Old Trafford. Then they had asked about Estela. Junk had told them he didn't know her. She was some Brazilian tourist, wasn't she? Mayhew said they had been unable to find her at the address she had given.

'So you went to find me instead?'

That was when Havers remembered to radio base: they had located Mr John Quay at the Howdam Street bar. Surveillance would no longer be necessary, either at his flat or his place of work.

Junk said, 'You had an all-points out on me?'

Mayhew said, 'We don't use that terminology. We prioritised you.'

Havers and Mayhew's new priority seemed to have something to do with the BBC van. They joined the crowd of uniforms and gathered around it, sharing coffee out of polystyrene cups. An older policeman, a Detective Inspector with a greying face and yellow hair, surprised Junk by asking if he'd noticed the other van in the corner. He pointed the way with the edge of a clipboard. Junk followed the line and saw a decrepit van, smaller than the BBC's.

'It's a breakfast television crew that arrived earlier. Actually, I'd say they were a bit incompetent. What happened, they knocked the satellite aerial off as they drove into the carpark. I heard they were still looking for a repair man.'

Junk said something, perhaps oh yes? He couldn't say for certain. He did know Detective Inspector Green.

'You know a bit about TV, don't you Mr Quay? Maybe you should help them. Once you've finished helping us with our inquiries.'

Junk nodded. Yeah. Perhaps.

DI Green's eyes were back on the television people. 'I tell you, it's been non-stop since about midnight. First the kid gets topped at your place. Then this Paki restaurant gets shot up. I tell you, it's a fucking nightmare. In the last ten hours, I've had to write five different press releases. Two of them were scrapped because they were already out-of-date. Another got binned because the people in DTP forgot to send copies to the Chief Constable and it was decided that if he hadn't seen it then no one else could either. We've got a press conference coming up in ten minutes and I've got no fucking idea who's going to present that.'

Junk hadn't heard of the DTP. He was told it stood for desktop publishing.

'You sound as though you're run off your feet, Mr Green. Have you made progress with the case?'

'We've found that the boy in the Gravity was transsexual. Traces of drugs in his stomach were discovered to be a commercial female hormone compound used by people in the process of a sex-change operation.' DI Green read the relevant information off a sheet he had clipped to a board.

Junk said, 'That sounds like news.'

'It was to his parents. His mother was quite upset. Actually, we were lucky there. We wouldn't normally get results on the tests so quickly. But when the doctor cut him open, he found a quantity of undigested pills in the victim's stomach. He must have taken them just before his death. That was useful because it gives us a tight window on the shooting. Of course, no one heard the bang but the music is so bloody loud in those places. As you'd know.'

Junk looked DI Green in the face. The man had been waiting for him, lurking in the carpark. His clipboard ready.

'You've been working the clubs for some time now, haven't you, Mr Quay? Looking at your record, I'd say you've been involved in the Manchester scene since you were fifteen years old. You were a fucking early developer. Although you seem to have slowed down over the past ten years. We've got nothing recent on you and what we do have is mostly possession of amphetamine sulphate.'

'I was a pretty heavy user.'

'You're not fucking kidding. You were a regular Billy Whizz. Looking at your files brought it all back. I'd just started working in Manchester, then. I remember there was a huge raid over in Rochdale, acting on information received. We thought we were going to find a European amphetamine mountain. But all we got were traces. Didn't we try and fit you up for something anyway, manufacturing or supplying or something?'

'I think there was an idea I knew more about it than I was saying. If I talked, they'd see what they could do. If I didn't, I'd be in shit.'

'Yeah, yeah, it's coming back now. Some of the cops back in the seventies, unbelievable. In a way, you had to admire them, they were total scum. I loved it when I was a young copper; it was like being in the middle of an American film.'

Junk wasn't so keen at the time.

DI Green turned his sheet over. 'Well you got away with it. No time in prison, psychiatric reports, that's it. They decided you were too unstable to give evidence. The shrinks said – what was it? I know I've just read it – serious psychotic episodes.'

Junk remembered some of them, not all.

'And you still work for John Burgess, who was the man we reckoned was behind the whole thing.'

Junk said, 'He's straight now.'

'Oh, forget it. Water under the bridge. I bet he's embarrassed by this shooting, though. That must spoil the spotless image.'

Junk wondered how long this would go on for.

'I don't suppose you know how we could contact Ms Estela Santos? We've had a couple of boys sat outside her place since early morning but without luck. We've staked out the airport, station, whatever. You wouldn't believe the amount of manpower we've put on it. Womanpower, too. Still, we've got the resources. That's one thing that's different to when I started. Now, just about every other person you meet is a copper. There are millions of us, I swear. You can almost imagine why the old coppers were such bastards, they were working themselves into the ground. Most of them ended up being thrown out or retired off, they were uncontrollable. You've got to laugh, I mean, we should have sent them for psychiatric evaluation instead of you.'

DI Green had a reputation as something of a throwback. Junk thought that he wouldn't have looked out of place with the police who used to work him over in the past, after 3 a.m. busts. He could almost taste the rubber-metallic sheen that came off the hoses as they laid into him. The rubber of the hose, the metallic smell of his own blood, streaming from his mouth or choking below the surface of the skin – without the skin ever breaking.

'This Brazilian bird is a mystery. It seems her passport is genuine but it has her down as a man. We almost didn't notice. In a sense the bureaucracy here is a blessing; Miss Santos's papers were checked so many times, eventually someone noticed the gender anomaly. Do you suppose John Caxton wasn't in fact transsexual? That he'd taken Miss Santos's pills by mistake? I suppose someone should get on the phone to his mum and explain that he might not have been a bender after all.'

Junk was taken to another room. DI Green had decided that whatever Mr John Quay chose to tell a police officer in the course of his investigations, it should go straight on to tape.

'It's more of a legal requirement, all this taping of everything, having it typed in triplicate. I tell you, the amount of initialling every scrap of paper received – unbelievable. But if it guards your civil liberties, Mr Quay, I think we're agreed it's a bloody good thing.'

Junk looked at the wall behind DI Green's head,

wondering if the matrix of cracks that ran beneath the white paint could map out a new strategy. Overlooked by Junk, DI Green's junior partner placed a clean cassette in the machine on the table and pressed Record. The tape had been running five minutes but no one had yet asked a question. DI Green spent the time shuffling through a stack of computer print-out. When he looked up, all he said was, 'They take some reading.' He flicked to the front sheet and tapped the title page. 'Burgess's record as an entrepreneur and nightclub promoter. All of it fucking hearsay. What they call inadmissable. But I can summarise.

'It was said, at the time, half the reason for Mr Burgess's success was that he used his clubs to launder money. There were rumours, as I recall. For instance, that he enjoyed the protection of a group of, shall we say, businessmen. What I would call old lags, slags and blaggers. But, so the rumour goes, by the mid-seventies the money came from drugs. Mostly from Burgess's own drugs. He was alleged to be the biggest supplier of amphetamine sulphate in the North West – and in those days, the whole of the North West ran on speed. Probably would still, if it wasn't for newer or more fashionable pills and powders, hey, Mr Quay?'

Junk tried not to look anything. Not even expressionless, in case that was taken as insolence.

DI Green barely paused. 'After pissing off the older guys because he refused to front for them any longer, and as a consequence of setting up on his own, John Burgess ran into some trouble – which he managed to contain thanks to the bunch of thugs he'd put on his pay roll. Chiefly, a white lad named Bernard Chadwick and a black called Michael Cross. Michael Cross was recruited off the Kippax at Manchester City, where he had a reputation as a football hooligan.'

The next pause opened out. Junk wondered if he should speak. His mouth opened but DI Green brushed it aside.

'That's okay, Mr Quay. I'm really only reminiscing, talking as much for myself and the young lad here,' DI Green flapped the sheaf of computer paper he was reading from at his junior partner. 'Where was I? Yes. By the time John Burgess got around to actually owning nightclubs on his own behalf, he had a secure business – based on locally manufactured amphetamine sulphate, known as 'speed', and locally produced muscle, namely black football hooligans and a crop-headed soulboy, the aforementioned Bernard Chadwick. Despite several police operations, we never found enough evidence to convict John Burgess of anything but minor infringements of the licensing laws. Although . . .'

DI Green began to run a short finger down a column of typeface.

'. . . you spent time on remand, I believe, before finally receiving a suspended sentence.'

Junk said, 'Suspended, yes.'

'And another of Burgess's associates, a Mr Paul Sorel, managed to disappear between being put on remand and going to trial. No need to keep opening and closing your mouth, Mr Quay. I'll tell you what you've got to say, when the time comes to say it. For now, I'm just nattering away. I tell you, sometimes I've got a mouth on me I just would not believe.

'Let's see now. Paul Sorel. He should have faced charges of dealing, just like you. But with him, there was more evidence. You were caught with about fifteen grammes of speed. Paul Sorel was caught with about sixty grand in soiled notes and he couldn't account for a penny of it. As I remember, our strategy rested on getting Paul Sorel to admit he was carrying the money for

Burgess, that it was to be put through one of his night-clubs as legitimate revenue. But this Sorel proved to be quite a tough nut, despite being an outrageous homosexual of the effeminate tendency.'

DI Green paused: 'How do you think that last phrase sounded, Sergeant? You've got to be careful how you phrase some of this stuff. But as none of this is likely to go as far as court, I suppose I don't have to worry too much about the public hearing how the guardians of law and order talk in unguarded moments.

'Let's see. Paul Sorel – total wooftah, camp as Christmas and a coon to boot. That about sums him up. The shirt-lifting fairy did a flit. Now here's my question, Mr Quay. Was Burgess pleased or dismayed when Paul Sorel disappeared?'

Junk didn't mean to say it. It slipped out: 'No comment.'

'Oh, come on. Did John Burgess know Paul Sorel? You can answer that.'

'Yes, he knew him. Paul worked at every club Burgess ran, like I did.'

'In what capacity?'

'Bartender, cloakrooms, door . . . anything, you know.'

'Accounts?'

'No comment. I mean, how would I know enough to comment. I did donkey-work, some DJ-ing. I wasn't management.'

'Was Paul Sorel?'

'No comment – well, I suppose you could say he was junior management.'

'So, he was a useful associate of John Burgess. Now the question again. Was John Burgess pleased or displeased that Paul Sorel did one, at a time when he was supposed to be in Risley remand centre?'

'How should I know. Pleased, I suppose.'

'Why? Because Paul couldn't testify against him?'

'No, pleased because Paul was a friend and wouldn't have to spend more time in Grisly Risley.'

'So they were friends? Doesn't that mean that John Burgess would be unhappy, because he'd lost a friend? Say, for instance, John Burgess had lost the closest friend he'd ever had and now Paul Sorel was gone, Burgess was weeping away into his lavender-scented pocket handkerchiefs. What would you say to that?'

'No comment.'

'Was Burgess broken-hearted?'

'How the fuck should I know? I'm not Burgess's confessor. What does this have to do with last night anyway? A boy was killed, that's all. Everything you're asking about happened twelve years ago.'

Junk was beginning to grow uneasy in his seat; the rub of the plastic seat through his trousers agitated his fleshless bones, the sharp points of his buttocks. Other sources of anxiety, besides the matt-plastic seat, were the web of lines on the painted surface of the walls and the painfully slow whirr of the tape machine as it ground through its recording. Junk hardly slept, but everyday textures assaulted him with the micro-intensity of a dream. If this were the old days, if this were the seventies, DI Green would have beaten him unconscious by now. Was that better or worse? Worse. Of course worse. When Junk thought silently to himself, and imagined two oppositional choices, he was amazed to find how often he would pick the lunatic's alternative. He would have to watch that, that kind of tendency could end up harming him in real life. Now Mr Junk, for the ten-thousand-dollar question: will you take the holiday or push your arm into a waste disposal unit?

'Mr Quay, John Quay. Are you listening?'

'Yeah. No. Fuck it, what is it now, officer?' Junk switched himself back into the room.

'Get it together, Junk.' It was the first time DI Green had used his name.

'Yeah?'

'Murders get solved quickly – or they cool until there's no longer any energy to the case. We want this solved. Everything we've found so far is heading off on a perv trajectory. We find a boy with his throat shot to pieces and enough oestrogen inside him to turn a bullock into a milky Friesian. We find him spread out over the floor of a club run by a suspected chocolate-stabber. Meaning Mr John Burgess. Well, it seems to indicate a pattern. Then a smart WPC with a smattering of Portuguese discovers that our central witness is a tranny and we think – whoa, hold on there, boy. I mean, the whole of Manchester might be swimming in a cesspit of its own making, as a great man once said, but this is all getting out of hand. Ms Estela Santos, which I guess is not his-stroke-her natural name, can't be located anywhere so I get a search warrant and by ten this morning we have his-stroke-her flat turned upside down. We come up with a used johnny carefully disposed of in the kitchen fliptop, a messy business. But the doctors down in the slab room are paid to handle that kind of thing and in no time at all they identify the sperm in the said johnny as belonging to our dead boy. The circle closes.'

'I don't see it,' said Junk. 'If Yen, John Caxton, had been with this Santos – then talk to her. I can't help, I don't know her.'

'But you do know John Burgess. You know him as well as anyone. And you also know this Caxton boy, or Yen as you just called him. And, as you know, this Yen worked for Burgess at his travel agents. What we've found out, after interviewing about half the space cadets in Manchester, is that Yen was halfway to being a moron. Still Burgess gives him a job. Not only a job, but something of a front-line job, a job carrying a whole lot of perks like cheap holidays and knock-down flights. Why? Had Burgess got some kind of special fondness for our dead boy? You tell me.

'Then we find that this boy has some kind of sexual identity problem. He likes to sleeps with men – or men-dressed-as-women. The sordid, swinging little circle seems to join up. That's the way it seems to me.'

Yen chanced it: 'Do I have to listen to this?'

'No. All you've got to do, if you're fed up of listening to me and all my reminiscing and speculative theories, is start talking yourself. Nature abhors a vacuum, and if I hear another fucking 'no comment' then I'm going to talk. Because I tell you, Junk lad,' DI Green leant over, stubbing his forefinger into the table, 'I've barely started.'

'You've been with Burgess since you were fifteen. You and Sorel were his original boys. You could say that Burgess was your mentor, your father-figure. Now another of Burgess's protégés turns up dead. You know this Yen boy well enough to use his street name. Know him well enough to let him hang out in your own private room at the Gravity. Know him well enough to show him your videos, too, I bet.'

DI Green paused; something had come to mind.

'Just to digress, we've confiscated every one of your videos that we found – both at the club and in your place in Hulme. There's a vice team working through them, even as we speak.'

Junk took in the information, registering it like an intrusion. But he let DI Green continue.

'To get back to the facts of our investigation – the way it seems to me, you are the one who connects Burgess with this Yen kid. Can you tell me anything that proves that you weren't procuring another generation of boys for

Burgess – now that you've grown ugly and Paul Sorel's gone AWOL?'

Junk said, 'Paul's returned. He's the Brazilian woman.' He left a beat, then added, 'Burgess asked him to come back.'

SIXTEEN

From his voice, you could tell Burgess was in control of things.

'Get that telly and put it up on the desk. You don't need to worry about the fucking aerial, we're not here to watch the fucking telly. Just hitch up the VCR, you gormless cunt. Bernard, tell me, are you ready to twat this bastard? Because I'm about ready to kick his twatting arse down the twatting stairs. Pissing cock-sucker ponce . . . I said, Channel Nine. We're going to watch a fucking video, so switch the cunt on to the video channel, cunt-breath.'

The boy finished, looking totally relieved to get out of the room and back to the bar. Theresa recognised him, but he'd got so hyped he hadn't let on to her. John Burgess had kept him somersaulting through a solid chant of obscenities. It was hard to tell if Burgess was angry; if it was habitual or if he even knew what he was saying.

Theresa had barely spoken since fat Bernard kidnapped her. Bernard hardly broke for breath. It was two hours now since she last opened her mouth. She only wished she had run when Junk arrived with the police, but she hadn't wanted to see them either. She hadn't realised how little she wanted to see Burgess, not until he showed. Now she was stuck, dead centre in front of the TV. Bernard blocked the door. Burgess raged about the room, waving the VCR remote like a stun baton and looking for his tapes. When he found them, he held them up. Two VHS cassettes, unmarked and boxless. Theresa knew she had been brought here to provide a voice-over.

Now Burgess spoke: 'You're a friend of John Caxton, aren't you? More than a friend – you were the first one by his side after he was shot. His own fucking Mary Magdelene.'

The tape began flickering. The tracking needed adjusting, although Theresa thought it would be stupid to offer. She wasn't here to clarify the situation. White bars of static rolled down the screen, obscuring her ghostly image as it wandered the balcony. She watched as it edged its way back to the room where she had shot Yen. She thanked it for not betraying what she was really feeling. Then it was gone, for just the time it had taken her to search through Yen's pockets and remove the stolen pills. She now knew they were hormones – she wasn't sure what. Female hormone tablets, like the pill, she supposed. Yen tripping off on birth control pills, it could have been funny, watching him explain that in the infirmary. Theresa remembered looking up as she took the pills and seeing the mess of his neck wound. There was an incredible amount of blood. She had felt guilty because she had tried so hard to avoid getting the blood on herself, her hands and clothes. As though, after killing Yen, there was a further crime in picking her way around the gore.

'Who killed him?'

Theresa didn't answer.

'Listen, cunt, who killed him?'

She remained still. Burgess nodded over to Bernard: 'Do something, scare her.'

'How?' As though Bernard hadn't been scaring her so far.

'Abuse her or something, let her know what will happen if she doesn't cooperate.'

Bernard walked over to her. Standing in front of her,

he called her a cunt. Burgess groaned, saying: 'Not like that. I've already called her a cunt. Don't abuse her verbally. Give her real abuse – you know, something a woman's scared of.'

Bernard looked over his shoulder, wanting some kind of clarification from Burgess. If he got it, Theresa didn't know. Burgess's head was obscured by Bernard's bulk. Turning back to her, Bernard pulled open the front of her blouse. Not tearing the material, but holding the cloth out so he could look down on to her tits. Theresa turned her head away. She felt a gooey wad hit the side of her neck. She thought, he couldn't have, not so quickly – she turned her head back to him involuntarily. He had spat, that was it. She felt the saliva as a wet comma on her neck, slowly extending as its tail slid down her blouse. She saw the residue of spit cling to the fleshy pink of Bernard's lower lip. Looking had been a mistake, he had her attention now. She looked at tired eyes, set into a head the size and shape of a pedal-bin – tired eyes, maybe bored, but unrelenting. Bernard moved a hand forward, his finger dipping into the gob of spit as it slipped past her clavicle. Bernard stirred it around, and then pushed his hand palm-down on to the enlarged wettened patch. Theresa could smell Bernard's spit. Sickened, she shivered. As Bernard's hand drove down to enclose her left breast, the shivering intensified. She couldn't stop, she was shaking.

'Who killed Caxton?'

Theresa tried to speak, Bernard could see that she was trying. Nothing was coming out. Her tongue thickened inside her mouth. She saw Burgess's hand go out and touch Bernard's arm. Bernard moved to one side, leaving his hand until he finally, slowly, pulled it out from the top of her blouse. Burgess was in front of her; the shaking would not stop. 'Okay,' said Burgess.

Burgess punched her in the face: 'Stopped now? Good. Once again, who killed Caxton?'

'The other woman.'

Burgess frowned. 'What?', then he saw that she meant the video. She was trying to look through him to the television set. She said it again, 'The other woman', and Burgess spun around and peered through the tracking static.

'That one?' His finger on the screen.

Theresa nodded.

'Where's that remote-control thing, Bernie?'

Bernard pointed; it was beside the television. Burgess ran the video back and forwards again. On screen, Yen's friend Estela was pushing down the balcony, opening every door as she came to it. The camera was behind her and the tape only gave a back view. The video reached the point directly after Theresa had removed the pills from Yen's body. Theresa watched the TV as it showed her come hurtling back out of the room, running from Yen's body for the second time. At the moment she barged into Estela, there was a fraction of a beat when Estela's head was half-turned. Burgess played it through again: rewind, review and cue.

'This woman?' He pointed, puzzled, at Estela's head.

'Yes.'

On the video, Theresa's face was the soul of horror. It could not have worked better. On the television screen, she looked as though she was scared of Estela: terrified only because she had collided with Estela.

'Well, what's she doing now? Going back for another look? She forgot her purse, what?'

Theresa didn't answer. Bernard was over by the TV set now. He pushed his face so close to the screen that the picture must have disappeared for him, reconfiguring as lines of pixels. He moved his head out and forwards again, trying to focus on the moment Estela's head turned. Burgess continued to move through the same scene, in both directions.

'Who is she, boss?'

Burgess was shaking his head. 'Who knows? No. No, wait a moment.

'I did see her, before. When she walked into the club. Pass me that other tape, Bernie.'

They huddled close to the telly. Theresa hoped she was being ignored. She tried touching her face with her fingertips to test the damage from Burgess's punch. She had hardly ever been punched before. Only once by a man, that was a teacher (ex-teacher, suspended and later sacked). What would a broken nose feel like? If the bone was flattened, surely the whole nose would push from side to side. If it was only cracked, would it still move? Touching the nose brought tears. She choked on them, but kept them silent. Bernard and Burgess were still bent towards the television set.

If her nose was fractured, would the swelling hold it in place for a time? Perhaps it would only flatten when the swelling was gone. Did that sound right? She caught herself just as a sob threatened to become audible. Bernard and Burgess were racing through a fast-forward trickle of men and women, walking through the double doors at the front of the Gravity.

'Stop. Stop.' Burgess was holding the remote-control himself. Ordering the video to stop while he jabbed at the little rubber button. 'Bastard. Ah, there. Just there.'

'That's a good picture,' said Bernard.

Estela stared, full-face, up towards the security camera.

'Well, who is she?'

'I don't know, chief. Does she look familiar?'

'She doesn't look completely unfamiliar. Who is she?' The question was thrown over his shoulder. He was looking over towards Theresa again.

'She picked Yen up, the night before.'

'That's John Caxton, right. She picked him up, when? The night before he died?'

Theresa felt a stab from her nose as she nodded.

'What was it then? A lover spurned, some kind of shit like that?'

Theresa said: 'She bought him drinks all night. Then she took him back to her place.'

'She some kind of paedophile? What is it?' Burgess's eyes were back on the screen. 'How old would you say she is, Bernie?'

'I don't know? Thirty?'

'I would have said older, what did she want with a prick like Caxton?'

Bernard said, 'His prick?'

'Well, it wouldn't be his fucking mind. Why did she kill him?'

Theresa guessed she was supposed to answer that one. She told him that she didn't know.

'He left her while she was sleeping and then came round to my place.'

'Did he say anything?' asked Burgess.

'He said he saw photographs of you.'

'At this woman's place?'

Theresa remembered to speak, not nod: 'Yes. She had photographs of you in a folder inside a suitcase or something. Different ones.'

Burgess thought for a moment: 'Then she's a journalist. Is that it? She was writing about the club for one of those style magazines?'

'She had a gun, as well. Next to the photographs.'

Burgess couldn't see it. Why would she have a gun?

'What else did Caxton say?' he asked. 'Did he tell you what she was doing in Manchester?'

'No.'

'There must have been something else said besides?'

'He said she was Colombian.'

Theresa saw Burgess whiten. She suddenly knew what 'blanch' meant, Burgess had totally blanched. He stopped, struck in mid-movement. Bernard was frowning, his brow crumpled as he tried to puzzle it out, staring at the frozen image on the television screen for a clue.

'Colombian, chief?'

'Hush.' Burgess silenced Bernard. 'Don't say anything.'

'She picked up John Caxton, though. Why would she do that? It has to be deliberate.'

Burgess said, 'It's got to be to do with the fucking travel agents, hasn't it?'

'Well, yeah. That's what I was thinking – he works there.'

'Then, after she's spoken to him, and after he's found out something about her . . .'

'She shoots him,' Bernard finished Burgess's sentence.

Burgess was nodding vigorously: 'Fucking Colombians. Fucking Colombian fuckers.' After each nod.

'What could he tell her about the travel agents?' asked Bernard.

Burgess was fucked if he knew. 'You tell me? Fuck all. Caxton was a fucking moron. What would he know?'

Theresa didn't hear the rest. The sirens had started in the street below.

SEVENTEEN

Bernard and Burgess looked out of the window. The rubberised squeals of car wheels and the wail of sirens must mean something. Bernard and Burgess had not yet worked it out.

'What the fuck's all that in aid of? They think they're in a fucking cop show or something?'

'Don't ask me, boss, I don't know. They're playing top wheelies?'

Burgess shook his hand at the window, his palm facing upwards and spread as he mimed incredulity. 'I don't believe that. A handbrake turn on a fucking one-way street. And what's with the sirens? They're not going to the raid the bar, are they?'

Theresa knew that the WARP hadn't been raided in months. Whenever it had been, the police had never found any drugs beyond light eighths of dope collecting dust in different pockets or pushed into the corners of matchboxes. The police no longer cared about dope and Bernard made sure that they never found anything else.

Bernard said, 'Let them raid it. This has got to be cleanest bar in the world.'

'Perhaps they've come to look for someone specific.'

'Yeah, maybe. That's what they were here for earlier when they arrested Junk.'

Burgess hadn't heard anything about this.

'Yeah, it was just about an hour before you showed. The cops ran in after John Quay and took him off.'

'Why the fuck didn't you tell me?'

'So they arrest him. It's their job, they arrest people all the time. If I was them, I'd arrest Junk – pock-faced, one-eyed cunt, he looks like a villain.'

'You didn't think it was significant?'

'Why should I give a fuck about John Quay?'

Theresa watched them bicker. She wondered if she could make it to the door and down the stairs while they argued at the window. They were looking down to the street again, now. Bernard was pointing, 'Isn't that DI Green?' Burgess stared out of the window. 'What do you suppose that cunt wants?' Theresa would have made a run for it in that second, but Burgess ordered Bernard downstairs.

'Go find out what they want.'

'What good will that do? I'm supposed to just stand there and ask them if I can be any help?'

Burgess took Bernard by the arm, pushing the bigger man towards the door: 'Just get down there, you cunt.'

'Okay, okay.'

Bernard's fat feet pounded down the stairs. Burgess went back to the window and, after a second, walked back to the door. He seemed to be unsure where to put himself. Another second, and he gave up. He reopened the door and followed Bernard down the corridor. Theresa heard him on the stairs, taking them quickly but coming to a halt around halfway. She listened as another set of feet climbed towards him and stopped as they met Burgess. More than one set of feet; there might be two pairs. She waited to hear what Burgess might say to them. When the voices came, they were not completely muffled. Burgess was asking if he could help. The voice that replied was saying: Too right, too right . . . something, something . . . something.

Theresa wiggled her mouth side-to-side, trying to feel for any damage to her nose. Perhaps it wasn't broken;

Burgess's fist had landed partially on the bridge, but he had really punched between her eyes. That was where the full force had hit her, that was why she had a headache. She stood up and walked over to the cupboard.

The television stood on the desk, a cupboard to the side. On the TV screen, Estela's face was paused, staring up towards her – the mouth slightly open, the head tilted backwards. Theresa had nowhere to go.

She couldn't run, not while the stairs were blocked. She could only hide. She looked from the cupboard to the desk. Hiding under the desk seemed pathetic, it wasn't as if she would be out-of-view. But the cupboard looked too small. She pulled at the cupboard handles and swung the double doors open. The cupboard was lined from top to bottom with shelves, leaving no more room.

Outside, the footsteps grew louder as they climbed towards her. She thought, oh hell, and scooted under the desk. If the doors to the cupboard remained open, she was almost out-of-sight. She brought her knees up to her chin, making herself as compact as she could.

Several sets of legs, cut off at the knees, came into the room – four pairs. Theresa recognised Burgess by his brown elasticated boots. The black Doctor Martens beside him stuck out beneath blue trouser legs. Theresa knew that if she traced those legs up through the cruddy suit they must belong to, they would end with a policeman's head. If the brogues belonged to a second, possibly younger, cop then the white hi-top trainers must be Bernard's. Theresa hadn't noticed them before. He must think he looked totally sharp in his Nikes.

The Doctor Marten-man was speaking as the crowd of legs moved through to the room: 'So why didn't you turn the tapes over to the police?'

Burgess now: 'We were conducting an internal investigation.'

'Oh yeah? On a murder? Does that come under staff problems, or what? The takings on the bar are down, the toilets are clogged and there's a dead body in the DJ box. This isn't Cluedo, Mr Burgess.'

'The tapes are here, Mr Green. No one was keeping them from you.'

'So I see. And look who you've got there. A good picture, too. Mr Paul Sorel; hard to believe, isn't it?'

'Paul Sorel?' Burgess's voice had gone up at least two octaves.

'It can't be just hormone tablets, can it? I'd say there's been some kind of plastic surgery done on the cheekbones, as well. And what do they call that stuff they inject into your lips to puff them about a bit? I know it's what that Madonna did to hers: cauli-gen. Looks like someone's given you a smack in the gob. Do you reckon he had that done as well? I know Sorel's been touched by the tar-brush but I would have said his lips used to be on the thin side. Those lips look ready for anything, eh? And that's a mouth made for big things.'

The Doctor Martens were right by Theresa now. This Mr Green seemed to be pointing straight to the television screen. She could hear a tap-tap-tap, as though he were indicating different features with a baton. Burgess was right behind him.

'Paul Sorel?'

Bernard's hi-tops were there, too: 'Sorel?'

'What a beauty,' said DI Green. 'I wonder what he's doing back here, after all these years?'

Neither Bernard or Burgess said anything this time. Their feet remained rooted to the left and right side of DI Green's Doctor Martens.

'Don't crowd me, boys, don't crowd me.' Bernard and Burgess moved backwards. 'Are those the rest of the tapes, on top of the telly? Right. Take those, Sergeant.'

The brogues moved forward, the hi-tops and the elasticated boots stepped out of the way. Theresa followed Burgess's boots around to her left, where they stopped. Something made her look up, following on from Burgess's boots until she reached his face. Burgess stared down at her, one eyebrow very slightly raised. Theresa looked back at him, sullen and over-stretched with fear. When DI Green next spoke, Burgess looked away without saying a word about Theresa.

'You want me down at the station?' asked Burgess. 'Why? You've got the tapes.'

'Yeah, I've got the tapes now. But there's a lot more you can help me with. Now that your old partner Paul Sorel's back on the scene, there's about a million questions that spring to mind.'

'Partner?'

'He kept the accounts, didn't he? Back in the days when you were speed-king of Manchester.'

'Fuck all that, I'm not answering questions on a case your lot fucked up twelve years ago.'

'Not quite that long. And now that Sorel's back, I'd say the whole case has been reopened.'

'You don't think I knew that was Paul? How am I supposed to recognise him when he's dressed like that?'

'Why not? He always had transvestite tendencies. Only now he's on hormone tablets, he's had his tits done. I don't know if he's gone for the final chop or not. Maybe that's another question I should ask you?'

'I'm telling you, I didn't know it was Paul Sorel.'

'Then why did you hold back the tapes – and why did you have this one paused, freeze-framed on his face?'

'Me and Bernie were looking at her – him. He was the one that was taken to the station with Junk, after John Caxton's body was found. I was interested. I mean, why shouldn't I be looking?'

'As part of your internal investigation?'

Burgess didn't answer.

'Well, you can explain all that down at the station.'

'And how do you want me there?' asked Burgess.

'In a squad car, I suppose. It's not as though we don't have the wheels – we aren't going to make you catch a bus.'

'I mean, am I helping with inquiries or am I under arrest?'

'Does it matter? These kind of distinctions are more bureaucratic than concrete. If I want you down the station, you're coming.'

'Then, excuse me while I phone my lawyer.'

'You're not getting nervous, are you?' asked DI Green.

'I'd say wary. If you want to conjure up some kind of tie between me and Sorel, now that he's turned up as a Colombian transvestite, then I want a lawyer on hand to remind you of my rights.'

'Colombian? He had a Brazilian passport when I spoke to him. Why do you say he's Colombian?'

There was a pause: 'I heard Colombian,' said Burgess. 'But Latin American, anyway.'

'It's funny you should say Colombian, though. I mean, Colombia being the place the schizo powder comes from.'

'If you're going to keep up with this shit, I'd better get that fucking lawyer down here now.'

'Don't worry. At the station will do, we're ready for off anyway.'

DI Green finished by turning towards the door. Waiting, while his sergeant ushered Burgess and Bernard ahead of him, and then following through. Theresa lifted her head above the desk and watched him disappear down the corridor. Then all that was left were footsteps on the stairs.

EIGHTEEN

'The taxi driver knew how to find you.'

'Yeah?' Michael rotated the joint so it burnt evenly, letting the smoke play around his lips, alternately folding and unfolding the bluish wisps with his pouting lower lip. The ash lay piled on a plate on his knee, among the remains of his goat curry. He didn't seem to have registered anything she'd said; the implied question, why are you so close to the Pakis?

He took another drag on his joint and held the smoke in his lungs. When he spoke his words were flattened, without the breath to round them out. 'What's this cabbie call himself?'

So, he had been listening. Estela tried to recall the man's name. 'Anjit?'

'Yeah, sweet.' Michael let the smoke flow across his lower lip, vacuuming it back like a waterfall trick-filmed in reverse. 'Amjad, yeah. He's all right. I met him through one of his cousins.'

Michael had style, but it was pure street style. Estela could not tell if he was reformed. He had never stopped dealing. He still had a pusher's insouciant front, with dark hints of reverse-side violence. She needed to know how Michael fitted into her astral scheme, the salad that fate had tossed together for her return to Manchester. Nothing was ever clear or straight when it came to destiny; fate could never keep a clean house.

Estela wondered how this would play: 'You are pushing heroin?'

'No fucking way.'

Why should she believe him? 'But the Pakistanis are still bringing it into Manchester. I know it's true. Why else would a couple of brothers machine gun that curry house? You can read all about it in the *Evening News*.'

'I don't read the paper, but I know Jabhar's place was hit. Yeah, some Pakis are bringing in heroin. Instead of the mafia or the triads or shit, Manchester's got its own independent trade routes. The golden triangle: Manchester, Bradford, Karachi. Pakis smuggle it over, niggers sell it. Whitey buy it. Sweet – but I've got nothing to do with it, and neither's Amjad.'

'How do you know Amjad's cousin, then?'

Michael's smile returned. She would not believe this. 'He's a top clothes designer – I'm going to be his super model.' Michael spun out the last words with a cute babyish stress that made it sound like 'Mo-khul'.

She arched a plucked eyebrow: 'Yeah? A catwalk queen?'

'You don't catch me mincing. I walk out like a man, maybe swing my butt a little for the ladies.'

Michael snuffed the joint at the roach and flourished a new skin from his Rizla pack, rolling the new joint as he spoke. 'You should see me on the catwalk, super-fucking-fit. Amjad's cousin is down with the seventies style: tight tanktops, Oxford bags and leather ankle coats. Also some terrace gear but that's more eighties. Old skool style, burgundy jumbo cords and crew necks. I'm a natural for it all.'

'So you started trading on your hooligan past?'

Michael shook his head. 'I was no hooligan, or not to everyone. You remember what it was like back then. It wasn't only the boneheads who sang 'Hey ho the lights are flashing, we're going Paki-bashing.' You could hear kids too young to even understand it, singing it in the playgrounds. We stopped that, we almost stopped it on the terraces. Why shouldn't he ask me to model the stuff – I'm proud of those days.'

Estela said, 'You built unity. And now brothers are shooting at Pakis with machine guns.'

'Yeah, well.' Michael trailed off to end with a shrug. He licked down the last insecure edge of a newly rolled spliff and lit up.

'You know who attacked the restaurant?'

Michael nodded, sure.

Estela waited, but he was not saying. 'Why ask me? Go ask your friend Junk – he gets his gear from those guys.'

'Junk's using smack?'

'Not smack. They don't just deal in heroin. Not enough profit, now heroin is strictly a minority taste. Mostly they're pushing coke, or crack. Junk gets his before it's gone in the microwave.'

Estela had not wanted to believe Junk could turn to heroin; that his moods were so dangerous they needed that kind of tranquillisation. But she knew why he bought coke. 'Junk's clean. He buys the coke for Burgess. He either runs errands for the boss or he waves goodbye to his job.'

'It's for Burgess? I didn't know that, I thought the bastard had gone straight.'

'He's given up manufacturing, I doubt that he's straight. I know he's got himself a coke problem he prefers to keep quiet.'

'If it's not a business to Burgess, it is to Junk. He isn't buying the coke, he's trading it for speed. Eighty per cent pure amphetamine sulphate. The same mix we used to push.'

Eighty per cent pure, that was too close to the old recipe and despite his appetite for the stuff, Junk had never learnt to manufacture it.

'How can Junk have got access to such high-quality gear?'

Michael had his suspicions. 'It's almost like he's still sitting on the last consignment, the stuff the police never found.'

Estela remembered a chest freezer stored in a rundown factory on the outskirts of Rochdale. She remembered the look on Junk's face when he opened the lid and saw the bluey-white sulphate packed almost to the rim. She'd had to hold on to him, otherwise he would certainly have dived forward. His mouth was already open, gulping for a taste. Junk was quite mad by then; explicitly, officially insane. The night they were arrested, she'd been put in the holding cell next to his. All night, she listened as he threw himself against the walls. For eight hours, he had raged solidly, thumping against the tiles.

Estela had been on her way to meet Burgess when the police picked her up. The van overtook her on Corporation Street. She had no hope of running, tottering along on stiletto heels in a red kimono and a Debbie Harry wig. When they hauled her to the station, Junk was already there. She wasn't told. She could hear him, screaming at the end of a cold corridor.

She was made to stand at a desk and watch as the duty sergeant catalogued her belongings; all her bits and pieces, the shoes and the wig, the stockings that could be used in a suicide attempt and so couldn't be allowed to remain on. Finally, the sergeant came to Burgess's money: three thousand twenty-pound notes, packed like four slightly ruffled Jackie Collins paperbacks at the bottom of her bag. He counted each note, painfully precise as Junk roared and gibbered in the background. Estela tried to tell him 'The man needs a doctor.' The sergeant just leered at her. The same sergeant that almost twisted her balls off during a body search. He said he had to check everything, just for the record. Her testicles remained swollen during the whole of her first week in Risley remand centre.

The money was the only evidence the police ever found; the drugs were gone. It was certain Burgess never once suspected Junk of stealing them. Junk may have been mad enough to try, but was much too mad to succeed. He would have died in the attempt; they would have found him where he landed, headlong in the freezer, legs rigid in the air and his head encased, dead by misadventure. It was inconceivable that a long-time speedhead like Junk could be peddling it, years later, a few ounces every week. If Burgess had the vaguest hint, he would bury Junk himself. He would stuff every orifice with sulphate and leave Junk to explode.

Michael put down his joint and took a square look at her eyes. He said, 'You've come back for Burgess, haven't you? That's why you want a gun.'

Junk had thought the very same thing. But it wasn't true. She had no idea who she was going to kill when she arrived in Manchester. Estela sifted her few words carefully. 'It wasn't my intention. It just appears that killing him has got tied in with my destiny.'

'Yeah, right.' There was a sarcastic underbite. 'It's not like I want to stand in the way of destiny.'

Michael stood and turned to her; the bite had gone. 'I say the bastard deserves to die for what he did to you. I've got a gun. If you take it – you can follow whatever star you like.'

Estela nodded her thanks. Michael left the room and she reached inside her bag for her compact, intending to spend some quality time with her cosmetics, maybe remind herself how much someone could change in twelve years. Instead, her hand closed around the plastic tampon case. The bullets were still inside. Why ever she had kept them, she did not know. They could only tie her in with a lost Beretta, tagged as evidence and sitting on a shelf in the basement of some police station.

She dug deeper and found the compact. Flipping open the lid, her face shone out of the convex mirror – oh baby, baby, baby. There was a woman. She stroked her lips with a brush dipped in mocha rouge and trimmed the edges with a soft chocolate pencil.

She was not designed for prison. Her friends, her contacts, her reputation, they had all protected her during the short prison days. Nothing could protect her at night when she lay awake, freezing under a single blanket as the wind sliced through the glassless window, heaving on the smells of shit and piss that stuck to Risley, shrinking into a narrow slit of depression. Wearing Y-fronts that fifty men had worn before her.

Michael and Junk both expected her to kill Burgess, but neither of them knew for sure what happened that last night, the very last time she and Burgess met. And the indirect ironic cold fact was that Burgess had kept her alive. She had been able to bear her time on remand only because she knew Burgess would have to get her out.

On the journey back to Risley, after her second preliminary appearance at court, the prison van was caught in traffic. Estela sat slumped inside, back to the tin wall, cuffed hands squeezed between her thighs so she didn't have to see the bracelets or the chain. Her head down so she wouldn't have to look at the prison officer facing her. When the van lurched into the air she was thrown forward. Even then, although she couldn't know for sure that this was her moment, her great escape, she butted the officer cold.

She must have been three feet above the Salford pavement when the back doors popped their hinges and the van crashed to earth. Michael Cross was waiting for her. He wore a stocking over his head but was grinning beneath it. She was in tears.

It had been Michael's idea to sandwich the van between two breaker trucks and use their tow cranes to rip it apart. His boys threw one chain through the van's windscreen; they attached the other to the back doors. When the trucks drove in opposite directions, the van swung wildly in the air until its back doors gave way.

Estela felt like Cool Hand Lucretia, stepping into her rescuer's arms wearing prison uniform, brown denim jacket and jeans. Michael had a three-litre Capri waiting (the most stupid touch, too flash and too frequently stolen to blend into the early evening traffic). He hid her until it was safe for her to meet Burgess. She found him in his new club, a cramped shebeen the police had not yet discovered.

She was still working on her lips when Michael came back in the room. He caught her puckering out of a tingling, squealing, long lipstick suck that gave the rouge a pre-worn veneer.

'You're dead beau-khiful you, are you a mo-khul?'

Estela turned, smiling up at the joke voice. The smile rounded off to a gasp when she saw what he had in his hand: 'Jesus-Maria, the sweet fuck's that?'

Michael was carrying a preposterous handgun. Clutched at his side, it hung halfway down his thigh.

'I don't know. Some kind of fuck-off gat.' He slid it around so that, as Estela took it, she could grasp the handpiece.

'It's a Luger – at leas' forty years old.' She weighed the gun on her flat palm, then released the magazine. 'Two bullets only. It don' look as though it's been cleaned since the war . . . where you get it?'

'Off one of my sons. I took it off him: he either had to let it go or shoot me with it, stupid cunt. I guess now he's saving for a Kalashnikov, or one of those flashier guns: Hecklers, AKs or something.'

'An AK 47 is a Kalashnikov. Can you buy that kind of weapon in Manchester?'

'I guess so.' Michael shrugged. 'Even the cops have found a couple of Uzis. Listen, if you want the kraut gun, take it. I don't want to see it again. The little bastard has probably got a new one – and he'll probably shoot me the next time I try and take it off him.'

Estela dropped the Luger into her bag. She would have to strip it down before she began throwing her weight behind such an unlikely piece of hardware. According to the newspaper report, automatics had been used in the restaurant attack. She might find something like that. Or at least a shotgun, perhaps an ex-Jamaican army Smith and Wessons. For now, all she had was a two-shot Luger and no chance of finding ammunition capable of fitting the anachronistic nazi gauge – that was her luck, and still she believed in destiny. She puckered again – a long, slow suck through her bottom teeth. There were other ways of viewing the situation. She had heard people speak of the Luger as a classic, a masterpiece of Teutonic engineering. She was a Brazilian citizen and the Brazilians appreciated German design enough to keep the Volkswagen Beetle in production. Although her only link with Brazil came through the specialist cosmetic surgeons at her clinic in Rio.

She smiled her thanks at Michael. 'Maybe you'd like to show me off tonight. Just two models vogueing their way around town, I know you'd love that.'

Michael did not look too anxious to be seen stepping out with her.

'But first, I want to go to the gym.'

Michael shrugged, 'The gym?'

'I got to work out. Do you think you have anything I could wear?'

'Clothes? Like a sweatshirt?'

'Maybe a leotard.'

NINETEEN

Junk shouldered the bin-liner through his front door, struggling to avoid tearing the fragile polythene on the sharper edges of the banister rail. It was heavy; he had not thought his video tapes would begin to weigh as much as they did. The police had just bundled them into the black bin-bag. The tapes that had lost their protective cases were probably smashed. All he could say, at least he had his videos back. They had not ended up in the viewing room, care of the vice squad. DI Green had returned the tapes, as he promised he would, immediately after they finished their talk on the mysterious resurrection of Paul Sorel as a Brazilian woman.

Junk told himself that resorting and cataloguing his videos could wait until another day. It had been a half-lifetime's work, collecting countless snatches of mondo television. Only half his life, so it could wait. He was not going to hurry and reconnect when the whole of his life had schizzed so wildly off-track in less than twenty-four hours. What then? What was he going to do? Escape?

Escape had a variety of virtues, Junk saw that, although none came without subtle complications. He had to weigh the options, whether to choose an internal line of flight or hop on an external flightpath. The outbound route would mean leaving Manchester and touching down in a different city, perhaps a different country. It would be a positive move, a concrete means of cutting loose from the gravitational pull of John Burgess. Escape into internal exile had nothing in its favour; it meant only that he would get smashed out of his head and barricade himself inside his flat.

On the alternative tip, getting wrecked meant losing sight of himself for a while. It would mean a break from being Junk. That almost swung it. He took a microscopic look at the possibility of just signing off on a tour of gaga land, but could not do it. These days his only recreational drugs were dope and alcohol and they wouldn't take him far on his internal flight. Eventually, he would resurface. He was committed; whether in self-loathing or auto-apathy he long ago made the decision and now he was stuck with himself. And there was, finally, one other reason to keep himself together: this whole business needed seeing through.

He could not escape, he would stick around until Theresa was out of the woods. But he would have to move. He couldn't stay in his flat and wait for either Burgess or Bernard to descend and begin his re-interrogation. Junk left the over-stretched bin-liner on his living room floor. Wherever he went, he would take the videos along, too. He climbed the stairs to his bedroom.

His packing began haphazardly. If any of the clothes he threw at the hold-all landed inside, then they could go. Anything that was too weak to make the journey from the wardrobe to the bag was on its own. Junk tossed his laundry to and fro across the bedroom, asking: 'Who's in? Who's out? Because it's a fucking jungle out there, believe me.'

No, no. Call off this whimsical trip. Junk re-routed himself. Screwing his eyes up for a moment's concentration, he gained control. Five minutes later, he had zip-fastened his hold-all around a few essentials and returned downstairs. By the time Bernard and his dogs got here, Junk would have gone to ground. He knew he had already lost his flat. When they found him gone, they would leave the door swinging on out-of-joint hinges. Within a few hours, the temple of Junk would have been desecrated.

A knocking at his door sent him wheeling around, facing the plywood and wondering if he should move. Would Bernard or Burgess knock? Whoever it was, standing out there on the walkway, they knocked again. Junk thought Bernard or Burgess might knock once, but not twice. He opened the door on to a skinny kid.

Junk looked him over: 'Who are you?' and looking him over again, 'Didn't you hang out with Yen?'

The kid nodded. 'Yeah.'

'I'd keep quiet about that, it's becoming a real problem – knowing Yen.'

'Well, I worked with him at the travel agents. Anyone can find that out, they could interview me any time. Can I come in?'

Junk tried to say that he was leaving. The boy stopped him. 'No. We have to wait for Theresa.'

The boy said his name: Cozy. Junk let him in, checking the walkway as the boy passed through. When Junk turned back, Cozy was already at home, scanning Junk's flat with interest, marking the amount of TV equipment around the floor and the photographic stills blu-tacked to the wall. Junk used the walls to storyboard his videos, working out their proper order in sketches and photo collages that grew like bacteria until the wallpaper was obliterated. Cozy walked beneath the pictures, as though he were in an art gallery or rustling through a comic strip, screwing his face as he tried to decipher the narrative thrust. He paused in front of polaroid snaps of a TV screen showing martial art manoeuvres, interposed with pictures of waltzing couples that Junk had lifted from a library book. A few sheets in the series had numbers across the tops and only a written description of the kinds of images Junk intended to weld into their place: bicycle crashes 105, tempest 36, girl-on-girl 275.

Junk watched the boy and told himself, there's something wrong with him. So far, all he had said was he got a call off Theresa, phoning through an address and telling him to wait there. Which meant that Theresa was safe. Either she was safe or the boy Cozy was setting him up. Another two fucking choices to ponder. Junk knew there was definitely something wrong with Cozy.

Junk decided he'd go for interrogation. He said, 'The police haven't spoken to you yet?'

Cozy looked away from the wall and shook his head. 'I skipped out of the club before they managed to round everyone up.'

'Why d'you do that?'

Cozy dropped his voice: it was the travel agents. 'I didn't want to answer any questions about it. The place is drowning in funny money. If the cops ever find out, I don't want Burgess thinking I was the one who grassed. Why should I care. I mean: so what? At least I've got a job.'

Junk finally got it. He knew what was wrong with Cozy: the boy didn't look spaced out. Watching him at the wall, Junk had seen real concentration, whole seconds of it.

Cozy dropped his voice to a whisper that left Junk craning even as Cozy bent towards him.

'But I been thinking, maybe I should have seen the cops. There was this woman who came up to me in the WARP and asked about Yen. This was, like, hours before he was killed. So maybe I should say something.'

'Why didn't you?'

Cozy would have shrugged, but in his embarrassment

only managed a sclerotic tic. 'I fancied her. And I thought she was coming on to me.'

Junk allowed a pause. 'That was no woman – that was Burgess's old flame.'

Cozy's mouth dropped: 'Oh shit.'

Theresa hadn't told the boy much at all, which was wise, Junk guessed. He had no idea why she had asked Cozy to meet her here.

The next knock brought Theresa. Junk took her to a window so he could look her over and see how badly she had been harmed. He told her the swelling around her eyes was temporary. There was no reason for her to worry about the nose, either. Everyone had to break their nose sometime. She was safe. For as long as he could keep her safe.

He said, 'You lost Burgess?'

'He was arrested, about an hour ago. I got away.'

'What about Bernard?'

She shrugged. She didn't know.

Junk said, 'We've got to go.'

The minute Burgess finished talking privately with his lawyer, the lawyer would pass his instructions on to Bernard. Burgess would insist that Junk be picked up: beaten up and picked apart. The facts were unravelling, the wheel was spinning, the chickens were back for a roost.

'Will Burgess still want me?' asked Theresa.

Junk did not know; he could no longer remember the plot he had been trying to construct for himself – the storyline that might at least explain events to his own satisfaction. He could draw a series of pictures and stick them to the wall, contemplate their sequence while he rolled a fat one. Then he remembered – he was losing this flat.

He said, 'We've got to run.'

Theresa wanted to stand around and talk. 'I know what Burgess's real business is.'

Junk nodded, Cozy had already said. It didn't matter, they had to go.

Theresa said, 'He's a money launderer.'

Junk nodded, he knew. It had always been Burgess's speciality, back when anyone who ran a club would keep the most perfunctory accounts and choose whether to add or subtract from the chunks of clumsy zeros on their bottom line. At audits, Burgess would claim two thousand people regularly visited his club. If anyone ever pointed out that his club only had a capacity of around three hundred and fifty, he'd laugh: 'What can I say? Most of them only stay five minutes. I'm going to have to sack the fucking DJ.' He would claim there'd been a huge take at the cloakroom or he'd held a raffle; he had the ticket stubs to prove it. A thousand different tricks, but that was then, and everybody knew that the Gravity was run with the ordered accounts of a public company.

Theresa said, 'It could be millions.'

Junk would have seen through the travel agency – if he had ever stopped to think. It figured, there had to be a dark core somewhere in Burgess's world, keeping all the other projects spinning in orbit.

'Don't tell me. Even if I cared, I wouldn't want to be told. And even if I wanted to know, there's no time now. We've got to shoot.'

It had to be the travel agents. Why else would Burgess believe Yen's death tied back to him, in some arcane way? Another piece of satellite debris careering around a black star. It didn't matter that Junk could not figure how millions could be put through a travel agents. Or where the millions were coming from. Burgess would know.

'I'm not interested – I don't ever want to hear. Now move.'

Junk slung his hold-all around his head, and took the bin-liner of video tapes by the neck: 'Come on.'

Theresa and Cozy picked up on the urgency and followed him on to the pre-cast concrete walkway that ran outside his flat, joining the block to its partners on either side.

'Aren't you going to lock the door?'

Junk looked from Theresa to his lost home – why not? He was not going to cut his own heart out, let someone do that for him. He threw her the keys and began to trot ahead of them.

He was the first to see the Lexus arrive with Bernard, Billy and the other bouncers. The four doors swung out from the saloon, bringing the four pumped-up meatheads into clear view. Junk threw himself back from the balcony, hoping he could not be seen from below. Weighed down by the polythene sack of tapes, he used his free arm to shepherd Theresa and Cozy up against the wall beside him.

'They've arrived.'

Junk had a top storey flat. There was no higher level they could climb to. Their best hope was to run over to a new block and climb down the stairs as far out of sight as possible. Four pairs of heavy feet echoed below them. Bernard's lot were heading for a staircase to their left. Together, Junk, Cozy and Theresa ran to the right. They kept on their toes, hoping their own echo was drowned by the clatter of bouncers below.

'The car.'

As they hit the foot of the stairs and started across a courtyard, Cozy was pointing to a yellow Marina ahead of them.

Junk said, 'What?'

'Over there. I've got a car.'

Junk hadn't expected a get-away vehicle. Cozy and Theresa were making straight for it. Junk thought, no. It was too out in the open. It would have been better for Cozy to pick it up alone and swing back across to pick them up. That would have played. Junk started after them, too late.

Bernard's shout carried across to them as they waited for Cozy to pull the security catches up on each of the doors. Junk threw his bags on to the back seat and climbed in. He had time to watch Cozy fumble with the keys for his brake-lock. He had plenty of time to watch Bernard and his boys run back along the walkway to the stairwell. Cozy fiddled with the choke and seemed to twist the gearstick in an over-elaborate manner, coaxing it into first. Junk wanted to scream, fuck the gearbox, just move. But he knew he needed to work towards a calmer rhythm – if he could hit the right plateau, he could maybe transport them out of this mess all together. It was a matter of field tactics, of hitting the right energy field and maintaining it.

Cozy managed to start the car before Bernard was out of the stairwell. This was the moment to decide – while they remained in a blind spot.

'Make for Moss Side and Alexandra Park,' said Junk.

'Are you sure?'

'Yes.' Junk's plan was to pass between two opposing fields, hoping they shorted out. Perhaps they could skate sideways in the confusion.

Cozy pulled the Marina across a kerbstone, heading towards Royce Road and on to Moss Side. As they passed back across Elmin Walk, now separated from it by a fenced-in playing field, Junk could see the Lexus start up. The chances were that Bernard had also seen them. There was no mistaking the yellow of Cozy's car, the colour of NY cabs and brick roads. Bernard must be singing.

Cosy slid the car on to Chichester Road. When the Lexus came back into view, there was no doubting – Bernard was gaining on them. Trashing the suspension against the kerb as they tracked around the bend by the school, the Marina was weaving like a motorboat on a strong swell. Cozy steered across Moss Lane on to Alexandra Road and Junk called the next turning. The Lexus was fifty yards behind them – ahead were the Moss Side dealers and their look-outs. Junk had reared up between the two front seats, he wanted to make sure he could see clearly when the time came.

The tableau ahead was an abstract arrangement of mountain bikes, splayed out across a field of road tar. No longer moving, the picture was frozen as every rider came to a halt and watched the cars burning towards them. The Marina was close enough to the bike riders for Junk to catch the details in their gestures. He focused: 'Steer towards the third kid, the one wearing the funny hat.'

As Cozy bore down on them, the riders began to move again, clearing a path for the careering yellow junkyard trash only twenty yards ahead of the black Lexus.

'Handbrake turn, now.'

Cozy hauled hard. The Marina seemed to jump through a hundred and eighty degrees. Junk flung open the door on the side away from the Lexus and dropped out – skimming his sack of tapes ahead of him. Junk was still rolling across the road as his tape collection scattered ahead of him, into the path of the cyclists.

Junk saw the rider he had chosen skid and fall. He managed to bounce himself upright, somehow, close by the fallen boy. He reached inside the boy's puffa jacket and pulled out the pistol. It looked like some kind of cowboy six-shooter. Junk hoped it was real as he thumbed back the hammer. The Lexus was stopped now, its nose inches from the Marina that lay across its path. Junk faced it down and began firing. The first shot went straight into the air. Junk kept to his rhythm. At the most, there could only be six bullets. Junk counted to five before firing again. The second bullet hit the top of the Lexus. Junk counted the explosion as his first beat, then it was two-three-four-five and he fired for the third time – aiming between the faces he could see in the Lexus's front seats. The bullet hit the roof again, but the Lexus was back on the move.

Bernard must have found reverse. The car shot backwards. Barely under control at that speed, it swerved madly from its back end as it wiggled on its backward track. Junk aimed for the road in front of the car for his fourth shot. The windscreen exploded ahead of him – Christ, could he have hit someone?

He counted, but didn't fire the fifth time. The Lexus had turned itself around and was fast disappearing. Behind his head, Junk heard clapping. He turned; the dismounted riders who were not clapping him were cheering. Junk stared half-vacantly around the group. About a quarter of them were holding guns. The boy he had taken the pistol from was right behind him, neither clapping nor cheering but keeping steady eyes on Junk. Junk switched the pistol from his right hand – where he had held it like a gun – to his left. Now he held it like a gift, offering it back to its owner.

Junk said: 'Er, thanks.'

The boy looked at his gun: 'That'll cost you.' The boy stared him out: 'Fifty quid in damages to the bike, three-fifty if you want to keep the gun.'

TWENTY

The newscaster paused, hand on her ear, listening to something that remained inaudible to her viewers. Her eyes refocused within the screen as she said: 'We can now take you to the scene of today's shooting in Moss Side.'

As the TV woman spoke, the pub emptied. By the time the channel had switched from the newsroom to the outside broadcast unit, the Croner Hotel was near deserted. The missing people resurfaced within the frame of the television, laughing towards the camera and throwing hand signals. Standing within a semi-circle of gawping youths, a woman with a microphone ran down the known facts to this latest Gunchester incident.

'At four-thirty p.m., here in Moss Side, a high-speed two-car chase ended in a hail of gunfire. A late-model, charcoal-grey BMW abruptly turned the tables on the executive class Toyota that had dogged its tail for three calamity-packed miles. According to information now in the hands of police, the BMW swerved to a halt at this very spot, outside the Croner Hotel, effectively blocking the path of the Toyota. In a dramatic twist the hunted became the hunter as gunmen in the BMW opened fire on the Toyota, without mercy and at point-blank range.

'The police are appealing for further witnesses to this latest instalment in the blossoming romance between Manchester gangs and their guns. At the moment, there is no confirmation of mortalities. Nor is there any certainty about the identity or the whereabouts of the group who carried out this lightning automotive attack. Both they and their BMW have disappeared into the unforthcoming shadows of Moss Side.'

Theresa had told Cozy to park in the carpark behind the Croner Hotel. As far as she knew, the Marina was still there. She didn't know what the nonsense about a BMW meant.

As the pub emptied, Cozy took advantage of the space at the bar. He was buying the third round of drinks that were supposed to ease their nerves. Junk gave him the money, peeling the notes off the same fat roll he had used to pay off the boy with the gun. Theresa didn't know how he came to have so much money. But there were other things she couldn't get her head round: either Junk's heroics or the adulation he got when he limped into the hotel. The men, mostly boys, who gathered around to shake his hand didn't leave him alone until the camera crew arrived.

Junk had barely spoken, then or later. Theresa helped him into the women's toilet and cleaned up his wounds but he still looked a mess. He had the same black eye he'd had before he flung himself from the Marina. His black eye matched her own. Now he also had massive grazing across half his face and his clothes were ripped down the left side of his body, exposing more grazes, road-burn and other scars. Theresa managed to pick out most of the gravel embedded in his flesh – she could not do much about the rest of the damage.

Cozy returned with a tray of drinks. He'd seen the news report and wanted to know why Bernard hadn't identified them.

Junk didn't seem to hear the question. Theresa wondered whether the fall from the car or the crack of gunfire had affected him. After the shooting, he'd paid the boy and begun an autistic hunt for his scattered videos. There were so many, and no longer anything to put them in. The bin-liner was in tatters, drifting aimlessly on the road like the twisted embers of burnt paper that float above bonfires. Theresa could not stop him, so tried to help. She threw as many cassettes into the back of the Marina as she could. The onlookers stole most of the rest. Theresa let them. She knew what the tapes meant to Junk but all she wanted at that moment was for them to disappear.

When the sirens started, she realised the tapes would have been evidence if Junk had left them in the road. By the time the Marina was parked and she and Junk were sat in the pool room of the Croner Hotel; nothing but Bernard's word could link them to the shooting.

'Why didn't Bernard identify us, Junk?' she asked.

Junk looked up, blanking on the question with a shrug.

'Will we get away with it?'

Junk said, 'Who knows. There were no witnesses.'

There had been twenty, thirty witnesses before the sirens started. But when Theresa had next looked around, they were gone. Those on bikes still seemed to be circling the car, but the circles were moving further away, the shock-waves from the shooting carrying them off in widening ripples.

The TV reporter signed off, the outside broadcast unit had finished filming. The studio-based woman delivered on an earlier promise and gave an update on the identity of the driver of the Japanese car.

'. . . named as Bernard Chadwick, head of security at the city-centre nightclub, the Gravity. Police refuse to speculate on a link between this attack and an incident that ended with the death of a young Manchester club-goer at the Gravity last night. We can confirm that John

Burgess, the owner of the club, is currently helping the police with their inquiries.'

Somewhere, a television camera was trained on Bernard's Lexus. Images of the car were flashed on to the screen. Close-ups of the roof showed a puncture in the metal where a bullet had partially penetrated the top of the car. The paintwork was grooved with long gashes, presumably the places where bullets had been deflected. The camera turned to the fractured windscreen. A lingering look inside the car failed to show bloodmarks, corpses – anything but tiny diamonds of glass.

The TV woman began to give the wider picture but had to struggle against the noise of people drifting back into the Croner Hotel.

'Today's incident in Moss Side is the third instance of gun-play in the past twenty-four hours. Although the police have so far refused to comment, speculation centres on Manchester's exploding drug problem.'

Junk could see the attractions of an exploding drug. He sucked at his brandy and ginger ale while he watched a series of camera-heads flick up on the screen for an impromptu vox pop.

'The police should have a curfew . . . they shouldn't be on the streets after, say, ten-thirty.'

'Do I think the police should be armed? Yeah, I think they should be armed. The police have to be able to maintain the violence on the streets.'

Returning gang members took up their seats around Junk, congratulating him again on the show he put up: the car chase, the shooting, it was mighty.

'Like Wesley Snipes, guy. I tell you, you were sweet. Top fucking action.'

Junk nodded; yeah, thanks.

One of them said, 'I know you, man. You're the Junkmeister. I'd heard these stories about you but I didn't fucking believe them till now. You're a monster fucking psychopath.'

Junk shook his head; no, no.

The boy wouldn't leave it. 'What I heard, you used to walk into clubs with a gat and take on every fucking comer. Blasting the fucking ceiling.'

Junk shook his head. 'I don't remember.'

Theresa looked over at him: what was this Junkmeister stuff? He was no longer as freakishly silent as earlier. He was still deeply spooky. When he screamed at Cozy to throw a handbrake turn, all she remembered was the blast of air as he launched himself out of the car. The next she knew, he was stalking Bernard's car with a gun in his hand. She could still see the way his arm spasmed with every shot. She had suspected Junk of many things but if anyone had asked, she would have diagnosed a more clinical, prozac-saturated and mundane psychosis.

'I don't remember that stuff.' Junk was shaking his head: I can't help you son.

The boy flashed him a shit-eating grin. 'Fuck. Keep taking the medication, man.'

He threw Junk a courtesy salute and turned to Theresa. 'You don't look too good. How d'you get the eye?'

The boy was solicitous, with a considered pout. 'Maybe you got concussion. You want to have a rest back at my place. Maybe check out some pain-killers from supplies while me and my brother look after you.'

Theresa said, 'Somehow, I don't think so.' But she looked over at the boy's friend. A younger model, startlingly similar with the same high forehead and deep dimples but maybe sixteen years old to his eighteen. Perhaps he really was his brother, literally, they looked so much alike.

The boy said, 'Don't worry, you'll be safe.'

The younger one smiled; he didn't look safe. Sure of himself, maybe. Like his brother.

Theresa gave them both a slow nod: really? Thanks but absolutely no chance.

The boy read the signs. 'You want to walk round looking like that, you got no shame, girl.'

'Excuse me.' She leant past him, excluding him with the gesture and with the blunt side of her shoulder. She asked Junk if he knew where she might find Estela later.

Junk said, 'Later? You should try the Passenger Club. She'll be with a man called Michael Cross.'

The boy pushed his way into the circle again, 'Hey, what do you want with an old fuck like Michael Cross?'

He had lost his dimples, his pout reduced to a sneer. 'Because if you see him, you tell him that I'm looking at a photo of his babymother – and she's wearing nothing but a big fat smile. You got it?'

Junk was giving the boy a look so sidelong it was two dimensional. 'Who told you that shit about me shooting off a gun in a club? . . . Was that Michael Cross?'

The boy wasn't saying anything.

Junk turned from the boy to his little brother. Weighing them together, he said, 'Michael's your father, isn't he?'

'Yeah, biological, like the fucking washing powder. But I've got nothing to say to him.'

'What's he told you?'

'What could he fucking tell me? I should get off the streets. Do time for kicking heads at soccer matches instead. What else? That I shouldn't touch drugs – unless it's selling dope. The man's full of shit. You know it.'

'Me?'

'Yeah. You've got the right idea. Do the fucking deal, whatever it is. You've not gone soft.'

'I'm not dealing,' said Junk, sounding surprised. Or was it wary?

'Whatever you say, man. If you say you're not dealing, you're not dealing. I've not seen you with the brothers. I've not seen the deals going down. I've seen nothing.'

'I'm not dealing.' Junk repeated himself.

'Sweet. Who is? I'm down with the Taz-Man and his posse and none of us are dealing. So what else did my old man say? All those stories about amphetamines. A guy ended up with full-blown psychosis. Who was that? When his nose and teeth couldn't take it any more, he started cranking the shit. He'd even shoot-up in his eyeball. Who do you reckon that was?'

Theresa knew this story, but she had never believed it was true. Perhaps it was; Junk did not deny it. He only returned the boy's stare.

'I didn't have to shoot speed into my eyes.'

'So why do it?'

The boy was leaning forward, Theresa leant alongside him. She also wanted to know.

'Everyone needs a gimmick. Like you with your gun.'

The boy opened his jacket: 'You're fucking tripping. I ain't armed.'

'I've still got one eye, I saw you pissing around with some kind of cowboy pistol out in the street.'

'While you were doing your demolition-man bit?' The boy gave the words a deliberate spin. 'Some guy might have passed a piece over. For all they knew, we might have had to shoot your mad white arse. You were flailing around, letting off shots in all fucking directions. It would have been a public service to put you down. Shoot out the one light you got in your fucked junky skull.'

'If you shot me,. you'd better hope I went down, After you'd pulled the trigger, you'd need both hands to help you crawl away.'

'If I shot you, you'd go down, man.'

Theresa knew the boy wished he didn't sound so petulant. Junk was relaxed, he was the one who looked like the dealer. Is that what he did? Is that how he had always had money for tapes and video equipment, why he had an encyclopaedic bankroll? Junk's good eye had glazed to frosty glass with that dead pusher's look. He listened as the boy threatened to shoot him and just nodded, asking if that was all he needed: just the one shot?

'You think you could keep from shaking long enough?'

'Like this?' The boy's hand came up from under the table. He had a pistol firm in his grip, the barrel only inches from Junk's nose.

Junk whistled, 'That's fast. Me, I'm a lot slower.' He stared the boy down as he reached around the back of his waistband.

'What the fuck you doing. You want a bullet in your fucking head?'

Junk had to squirm around in his chair before he brought his hand up, holding his pistol in a clumsy grip. But he never took his eye off the boy.

'Put the gat on the fucking table, man.'

'Later.' Junk took his time levelling at the boy's head.

Theresa was between them, looking sideways at two overlapping barrels, pointing straight at two noses. Ahead of her, the face of the boy's kid brother was freeze-framed. He couldn't have looked worse if the guns were aimed at him. She couldn't move.

Junk said, 'Your dad's a fuck-up, and I'm a dealer? Is that what you're saying? And you weren't impressed by the way I saw off the Lexus earlier. Is that right?'

Theresa felt five fingers flutter on to her leg and grip her thigh: Cozy. She heard his breath catching in asthmatic gulps. Ahead of her, the kid brother wasn't even breathing.

Junk's voice kept to the same pitch. 'So the next time I

do it, I should throw in a somersault, maybe put in a half-twist as I come flying out the car.'

She could count off the beats on Cozy's heart. But when the boy spoke, she could practically hear the grin.

'That might work. It would have got a round of applause.'

The tension was gone. As soon as she was able to break her gaze, she saw Junk's gun lying on the table. The boy laid his own next to it.

'My dad always said you were good value, if anyone wanted weird entertainment.'

Junk smiled. 'Did he say anything else?'

'About you, or what?'

'About a boy called Paul?'

'Paul Sorel. Yeah, I heard he was a batty boy, but he was also a friend of my dad's.'

'What else?' Junk sounded almost desperate. 'What did your dad say about John Burgess and Paul Sorel?'

'One thing. Paul was pulled out of prison, but he had to go see Burgess. When he got there, Burgess tried to rape him. Dad said one day Paul would come back and kill the bastard.'

TWENTY-ONE

Michael was already changed, legs apart in a corner of the gym, reaching down his calves until his outstretched fingers clamped on to his ankles. Estela stood in the doorway of the women's changing room and watched as he warmed and stretched his muscles, his buttocks riding high in the air.

This was Blue's Corner, one of two gyms on Moss Side. The other was run on slow municipal money but ran to a moderate swimming pool, a couple of squash courts and a weekly aerobic class. Blue's Corner had nothing but a ring, a rack of tarnished weights and a few home-stuffed bags hanging from hooks. The hall might have been large enough for fifty aerobickers if the ring was dismantled, the bags slung off their hooks. But it would never happen. Blue's was a more single-minded place: it dealt only with fighters, although not exclusively boxers.

Michael Cross would have preferred to take Estela to the municipal sports centre. He lost the argument. She made him confess: Blue's Corner had a women's changing room, and women weren't unknown there. True, the changing room was small, nothing but an afterthought. But when they arrived, two other women were working out. Both teenagers, both of them Thai boxers.

The Thai boxers were taking turns side-swiping a bag with roundhouse kicks, one holding it steady while the other let fly. Over by the weights, an elderly Ukranian, huge and bulbous, stood over a youngster and spotted him through a series of bench presses. Estela recognised the old man from 1970s Saturday afternoon wrestling specials, broadcast from Preston and used as fillers during the summer lulls at the end of the football season. Back then, he had worn a gold lamé leotard and spangly tights, making him look like a fat drag queen after a night entertaining dockers. But his opponents had looked the same so no one ever commented.

There were no mirrors in the gym's main hall but Estela had looked herself over in the cracked shaving mirror tacked up by the shower in her changing room. The lycra one-piece that Michael had taken out of Josette's wardrobe almost fitted her. Where it rode up her crack, she hid the damage beneath a pair of jogging trousers. Like the training shoes on her size-nine feet, the trousers belonged to Michael.

A group of men jolted through the swing doors at the bottom of the gym, all four wearing similar outdoor clothes, all in black. They had a leader, a short-set brother with tramlines across his hair and a bubbling shaving rash gnawing at his neck. He strode the length of the hall, giving the two girls a swaggering ballsey curtsey but passing straight by everyone else. A couple of his boys were less chill. They grinned over at the Ukranian, who saluted them, and stopped when they reached Michael, putting their sportsbags on the floor to swap hand-slaps. From where she stood, Estela heard Michael greet them by name and ask, 'How's it going?' The boys laughed, 'Business is kicking, know what I mean?'

Their boss turned round. 'Don't be discussing my business with anyone.'

That had them running off, their sportsbags swinging emptily at their side. All four disappeared into the men's changing room, opposite Estela.

Two bantamweights had got up in the ring, both of them naturals at the weight but upwardly mobile with good muscles. They began dancing round each other, not so much sparring as showing out a range of moves. One would lead with a right, the other would see it coming and swerve. Then they took an about-face and repeated the manoeuvre. Estela stepped out and took a tour of the ring. One of the bantams gave his partner a nod. When they broke off to look her over, she lit them up with a wink and turned her tail.

Michael had come up behind her. 'You here to mess with other people's schedules or do some work?'

'Okay, let's work.'

She dropped her hands to her hips and rotated her neck, scanning the room without breaking her exercise. 'Nice place.'

Michael said, 'You've been here before.'

No, she hadn't. 'I never used to keep myself in shape.' There had been nothing to keep in shape. Back then, she relied on late nights and amphetamines and she had kept herself thin.

Burgess had run a troupe of freaks, all of them wired on the speed they made themselves. All of them hooked into different circuitry. Bernard Chadwick had his own lunatic weight-loss programme, salting his potato chips with sulphate and downing them with pints of Snakebite. Michael lived out an obsession with Manchester City that was one part fashion parade, one part guerilla war. And there was Junk with his alarming turns. It was a fact, she had been the closest to normal. Burgess was, perhaps, the worst. He was always frazzled and rarely slept. Each morning, the fading of the streetlights became his excuse to telephone and tell her she was Number One, she understood the pressures he was under . . .

No, without doubt, Burgess was the craziest. Absolutely no doubt on the night Michael drove her to his office. Burgess paid the outstanding half of Michael's fee with hands that would not stop twitching. Once Michael had left for the bar, the twitches spread to his face until his face swarmed in a mass of spasms and contortions. He wouldn't hear a word, he could not take a refusal.

Estela shook herself out, bouncing on her toes and feeling the clinging weight of her breasts as they loosened and re-aligned themselves inside the tight lycra leotard. Michael stood in front of her until he realised exactly what he was looking at and hurriedly turned away. She followed him to the free weights.

'Who were those men you were talking to?'

Michael shook his head, as though he was clearing it. 'No one.'

'They your neighbourhood gangstas?'

'Yeah, so they think. The one with the tramlines calls himself the Taz-Man.'

She thought, cute name. 'Am I going to get to see them?'

'I'm not introducing you.'

'Who asked? What I mean, am I going to see them stripped down, working on a sweat?'

Michael looked disgusted. 'I'm not your fucking pimp.' He grabbed a pair of dumbells and began working on some swift reps, half-turned away from her so he missed her grin. 'Anyway,' he said, 'They're not here to work out.'

Estela got herself a skipping-rope and slipped into her training rhythm. Ahead of her, skewed on a makeshift ledge, was a TV set she had never noticed. On-line: a flustered blonde with a microphone and chequered suit, teetering on bow-fronted shoes as she asked passers-by for their opinions on God knew what. Estela kept her eyes ahead on the two bantamweights. She found, the faster she skipped, the slower they boxed. It was some trick.

From out of the men's changing room, she heard the

Taz-Man say, 'We on tee-vee? Crank up the volume on that motherfucker.'

One of his boys came loping out of the changing rooms. He reached up to the shelf for the remote control and whacked up the sound. Mutton Woman was asking about fear and the current situation; whoever she dragged on camera agreed there were reasons to be scared, currently.

The boy caught sight of Estela as he turned. He could hardly miss her, skipping in the centre of the hall. And she never missed a beat, running through three different steps in lightning time. He may have come over, his grin anticipated some kind of move, but he was called back to the changing room by his boss. The smile turned into a promise. Later.

She was skipping purely for the bantams when a tiny man in a pork-pie hat stopped play. His head stuck through the ropes, he started bawling them out, saying, 'Who told you this was a fucking dance class? You wan' sweet-talk wid each other, you do it on your own fucking time.'

The little man soon had them speeded up, the crosses and dodges became more real. Estela slowed her own pace a little, wondering which of the two would connect first. The man was shouting 'Work him, work him' but she didn't know who he was coaching, maybe both, without discrimination.

She had no interest in the television. She barely glanced at it. But then she heard an announcer name Bernard Chadwick and looked up to see the car he had used to kidnap Theresa, mounted inside the TV screen in wide-angled and foreshortened relief. The Lexus was scarred now, its complexion defaced by bullet holes and broken glass. Estela could not begin to guess what it was doing there, semi-derelict against a Moss Side street. But whatever cloud of bad luck Bernard had run into, she knew it had something to do with Junk. She once cast Junk's chart; she knew what kind of hapless star ruled his life.

The television trailed stills of the shot-up restaurant while a voice-over audited the damage. This was the report the Taz-Man had been waiting on. Before the end of first dissolve he had marched his posse out into the gym. A shade self-critical, he nodded at each of the pictures as they flashed by. But he took his bows when his boys began whooping his achievement.

The whoops grew louder throughout the report. At first, the boxing coach had only rubbed nervously at the back of his pork-pie hat. Now, he stopped the sparring session with a bark and signalled his boys to get out of the ring. As they slid through the ropes and made for the changing room, he kept between the Taz-Man and his two fighters like he was shielding them with his body.

The following news item had nothing to interest them. The Taz-Man turned away, and found Estela. She had stopped skipping but she didn't return his look. Up on the TV set, side view, cropped and framed, there was a photograph of Theresa. The picture appeared to have been lifted from a video. Theresa was recognisable but nameless. The newscaster was telling her audience that the police wished to interview this woman.

The TV was muffled by the voice of the Taz-Man, calling out to the two Thai boxers. Estela tried to catch the last of the report but only heard the newscaster sign off: 'In a prepared statement, the Chief Constable said that Manchester owes its police a vast debt of gratitude for holding the line against the forces of crime and, when an incident does occur, reacting with speed and professionalism on behalf of the city they serve and protect.' Then nothing more before the adverts.

The Taz-Man hadn't been idle while Estela watched

the TV. He had persuaded the boxing girls to take it to the ring. As they walked by Estela their heads were tilted together, floating whispers over indecisive giggles. The Taz-Man stood waiting for them inside the ring. One girl swung her way through the ropes. After stripping off her arm guards, the other joined her.

The Taz-Man got between them, saying, 'You gonna fight clean or you gonna do it dirty?' He held out his arms as though he were the only thing keeping them from tearing each other apart.

His posse hugged the sides of the canvas, shouting either for Fidelia or for Michelle. The girls touched gloves, retreated and moved forward. The first kicks were puppy dogs, slapped down easily. The Taz-Man slunk around them, playing the referee, air-kissing their hard round butts.

Estela found a place at the edge of the ring. She watched as one girl threw a couple of punches, recognising in her stance the shape of the combination that would follow. The defending girl blocked to her front and the attacker tried to catch her out with a kick to the ear. It had no hope of connecting, telegraphed from so far down the line.

Estela counted the aborted manoeuvres. The two girls were so familiar with each other's style, it was impossible to tell if either would ever cut it, full contact. She hoisted herself up to the ring. A second after she spoke, all action stopped. 'Why don' I have a go? I'll take either or both of you.'

The girls were staring at her, too unsure, their arms swinging at their sides with the weight of the gloves. The Taz-Man was for it, 'Motherfucker. Bitch is game.' Around the skirt, the Taz-Man's posse began beating afresh on the canvas, whistling up to the ring.

Estela slipped under the ropes. The Taz-Man met her,

ring centre, his hand on her backside. 'Which one'f you bitches going mix it?' The two girls had reverted to attitude, sneering at Estela like they didn't mind which of them put her down on her fucking arse.

Everyone heard Michael roar, 'She's not fighting. Get out the fucking ring, Estela.'

The Taz-Man couldn't believe it, 'You what, guy?'

'Out the fucking ring, Estela. Now.'

Estela shook her head. The Taz-Man said, 'Don't look like your bitch is going anywhere, Crossy.'

Estela leant into the Taz-Man's encircling arm. 'Maybe I should fight him, instead.'

The Taz-Man was pure grin. 'Yeah. Fight him.'

Michael stopped in his tracks. 'No. No way.'

Taz-Man wanted to know exactly how pussy he was.

Estela said, 'Come on up, Michael. Let's have some fun.'

'I'm not doing it. I asked you, now, get out the fucking ring.'

'We don't have to fight. Put on the arm shields, help me practise a few kicks.'

Michael looked down at the red padded shields the girls had left by the ring. He hesitated, but he picked them up and climbed up to the ropes. He said to the Taz-Man, 'Give me some fucking room, man.'

The Taz-Man followed the two girls out of the ring, saying, 'Don't go hurting yourself, Crossy.'

Michael slipped his arms into the shields and took up a position, forearms covering his body. Estela let a kick fly almost before he was ready. He blocked it firmly. Estela bounced back into position, smiling. The Taz-Man and his posse were clapping, 'Motherfucker.'

Michael knew she could have crushed either of the girls. He was blocking everything she threw at him but he had problems: the worst, making it look as though he wasn't trying too hard, doing nothing but stroll round the canvas. Way below, Estela could hear the Taz-Man urging her on, telling her to lay the motherfucker out.

She gave him three from the left leg, each of them launched in a side arc and all aimed at the same height. The trick was the speed, but it was really only a trick. They were easy enough to stop. She delivered the fourth with a feint from her right leg, but Michael saw through it. He put it down with the same economical gesture he'd used for every earlier one.

Estela sprung back with another roundhouse but this time she followed the feint with a punch to his face. His head snapped back, his defence way out of line, waiting for a kick that never arrived. In the tenth of a second he took to shake off the punch, Estela had swivelled to her left. All he saw, she was no longer dead ahead. Then a back heel smashed into his ear and he staggered on to his knees.

It took Michael longer to shake it off. His head swung from side to side only half a beat out of time with the jackal laughter that echoed round the hall. He was ripping the shields off his arms before he had time to think it through. Up on his feet, he was ready to punch her out. Estela waited. She had a smile ready for him. She had a bounce in her that set her breasts into locomotion.

She saw the look pan across his face, a slow-wipe as he realised what it would look like. He would be trying to stomp a woman, and he wouldn't even be able to do it cleanly.

He turned his back and climbed out of the ring. The Taz-Man was waiting. 'Nice. Nice, Michael. Now you know why your sons are down with the ConCho. They want a positive role model for the hood. Someone like me, stead of Daddy pussy, whipped by a bitch.'

Michael shrugged past. But the laughter followed him.

TWENTY-TWO

The Passenger Club was a large square room, a one-time sports hall. Around the size of a basketball court, with its bleachers removed, the club was overlooked by a high, wide stage. The DJ stood at its summit, the lower edges were filled with people dancing, throwing poses – some of them simply talking. The music was lover's rock, perhaps some jazz-tinged hip-hop loops every now and again. Soon, all those softer tunes would come to an end, Theresa knew it. They were the low-key preliminaries. The volume was still way, way down. The wheels of disco lights above the dance floor turned listlessly. But the place was totally rammed and everyone was counting the beats until it ignited.

Theresa felt over-dressed and heavily white. Clutching a duffel bag the size of a sack, she was jittered. She had been to the Passenger Club before. A few years back, she was as likely to go there as the Gravity but recently the city had begun to redivide, like an amoeba that can't flow in two directions without splitting its heart open. Techno and its derivatives, musical and chemical, had got paler. Her friends, acid casuals and ravers, had begun to shun hip hop. It was a question of space; other-worlds against the inner-city. When ragga re-ignited the dance halls, they left that alone, too. It was too, too heavy. Let its bass heavy lines work on the asphalt, techno's electronic bleeps were communicating with the solar system: black holes and white space.

Now she was deep into the Passenger Club, she found

herself looking for an easy ride between the two scenes. Wherever she went, these days, there was little that remained sexy about Ecstasy. At once mellow and energetic, every tablet either undershot or overshot the sexual moment. In the Passenger Club, the lust-in-waiting was tangible, it just about dripped off the walls. She could smell it around her but found it difficult to get a grip on its single-mindedness. Sometimes, its insistence sounded less than erotic and closer to pure braying, hardened to ambiguities and afraid of catching itself slipping.

Theresa was conscious of Cozy's left shoulder brushing against her right. He hadn't gone so far as holding her hand, but he was staying close. If Yen had been with her, he might not even notice he'd stepped out of their usual world. Yen's gift, his unnerving stupidity, meant he could go anywhere. Theresa had hoped that Cozy was straight out of the same mould as Yen, but he wasn't. A night and a day of murder, car chases, shootings and theft had left him quiet, and quietly trying to cope. If he had been Yen, he'd be skipping across the dance floor. He'd be up among the dancers on the stage, totally out of control and urging the crowd to get on One. He would slip amongst the black string vests, lycra dresses and pin-rolled trousers without a thought. Yen would never have noticed any reason to worry.

Theresa turned to Cozy: 'Are you okay?'

He said that he was. 'Yeah, fine. I can wing this.'

He hadn't denied being nervous, though. It was one more way that he proved he wasn't stupid. He knew when to hide what he felt and when to open up. He knew enough to act stupid when he worked for Burgess. Still, he had seen what was going on – he knew where Burgess's profits came from. He knew it wasn't from selling package deals to Corfu. Theresa touched his arm softly.

It hadn't been easy for him but he had stayed, through it all.

She had waited until they left the Croner Hotel, and then she had told him. They were going to break into the travel agents. They were going to ransack all its files, they were going to clear it out. Cozy had grown paler, his lips thinned out to pinched white lines but he had finally agreed. They were his fingers that skipped across the keyboards, sifting through security-coded computer files. She wouldn't have known how to access them, or even guessed what they meant. While Cozy worked, she stood around, eyeing her reflection in the blackest parts of the VDU screen. She thanked Jesus that he wasn't stupid, but she wished to the razored tips of her nerve ends that he felt a little of what she was feeling.

Now, with the job behind them, he had eased off that exact neurotic pitch. Inside the Passenger Club, he was just plain nervous. Theresa, on the other hand, was edging up to another note. She could feel it buzzing inside her. She hadn't quite got to it, that's all.

The wad of computer print-outs and counterfoils in her duffel bag were growing heavier, as though they were absorbing all the sound, the atmosphere and the sweat of the Passenger Club. She wouldn't have to hold on to the stolen files much longer; let Estela have them all. Buried somewhere within them was the story of the Burgess money-laundering operation. Through all the information that Cozy had selected from the travel agency's computer, were traces of Burgess's illicit deals, from lost ten grands to the odd fifty thousand pounds, all of it spirited from one country to another while Burgess creamed off his percentages. 'It's all there,' Cozy had said. Theresa had been too excited to listen properly as Cozy tried to explain the scam.

The weight of the bag was making her perspire at about ten times the normal rate. Clutching it tight, she may as well have taken a set of suitcases into a sauna. At the door to the Club, the bouncer had asked her, 'What's this? You doing your homework while you're here?'

She had shaken her head. She would have passed by him but she thought to ask if he knew Michael Cross. Would he know where she could find him? He looked down at her, saying, 'He's not here, love. Maybe later, you'll find him upstairs. With the other old men.'

She pushed her way through the dancers, swivelling around their sashays, knowing Cozy would hold fast to her tail. Whatever she was feeling, it hadn't spread to him. He was getting over it, getting over it, getting on. He wasn't looking for anything new. He hadn't got the biggest best fucking kick out of breaking his way into the travel shop. He hadn't gone for it with enthusiasm. And so, now it was over, it wasn't like he'd wrung himself out and landed in post-orgasm limbo. For certain, he wasn't thinking that he was maybe ready for more.

When they arrived at the travel agents, Cozy barely spoke. She never stopped talking, hot and breathless but unsure what they were going to do next. They cased the shop, front door and back. They ended sheltering from the rain under a tree in the old churchyard on Cheapside, staring across at the pictures of Balearic Islands and Miami winters that filled the unlit window opposite. Before they made their move, she wanted to test Cozy's knowledge of the shop, to make certain that it was enough to work on. While she questioned him, they shared a joint. She had bought it, ready-rolled, inside the Croner. The burning end fizzed like a sparkler as the cocaine sprinkled amongst the dope flared up.

She forced her way inside the shop via a glass half-light over the back door. It was the only alarm-free window, so narrow and dangerous, it had been overlooked when the security was installed. Or so Cozy believed, and he had been right. Theresa stood on his shoulders to attack the wireglass with a chisel. Once the window was smashed, she had to chip out every tiny piece of protruding wire. Cozy trembled below her.

Through the window, there was no way to go but down. She hung, almost all the way through, knowing that when she dropped hands-first to the floor, the first thing she would find were the fragments of splintered glass scattered below her. She pulled the sleeves of her jacket as far over her exposed hands as she could. She dropped. The pain was terrible, but it was in her shoulders and her arms and her back as she took the jolt of the fall. Only the tiniest of gouge marks bled from her palms.

Cozy's face was at the window. He was pointing towards the alarm box on the wall, where he said it would be. She took the flashlight he passed down to her and shone it on the box. He couldn't remember the exact code, but had used it often enough to picture the sequence in his head. He chanted the instructions down to her, 'Middle row, end button . . . top row, first button . . . same button again . . .'

There were eight numbers. Cozy only paused once. She saw him up at the window, pushing imaginary buttons in the air before he said okay. She tapped the last two digits and the flashing light at the front of the box went out.

Cozy used her chisel to break through the lock on his side of the door. Once inside, he took the flashlight to guide her through to the front of the shop where they both hoped the free-standing racks of brochures would hide the light from Cozy's terminal. He fumbled on the floor to reach the plug socket and switch his computer on.

Cozy worked nervously, efficiently; as though he were

trying to channel his mind on to the roaming green pixel-figures and forget exactly what he was doing. She had tried watching him but found her eyes drawn deeper into her own reflection. She saw her reflection, again, in the washroom mirror when she began to wash her hands and pull out the stray bits of glass. Her pupils dilated, her swollen lips carrying a frosting of sweat; all of the signs. The way she had bullied Cozy, the hours of anticipation, the way she felt as she cut herself loose from her fear. All of it like continuous foreplay . . .

She could imagine pulling him away from the key board. Bearing down on his mouth with her own open lips. She could imagine the indecency of being naked, there on the shop floor, as the different colours skidded across her white flesh, the lights of the computer, the amber of the street lights. She felt the blood swelling at her crotch, pumping out the folds until she couldn't even think of closing her legs.

And looking at Cozy, hearing the damp tap of his fingers on the keyboard, she had known absolutely that he wasn't anyone that she could get it on with.

He was still with her, here in the Passenger Club, although there was no call for him to be. Theresa bit down on a headache caused by too much excitement and only an uncertain end.

TWENTY-THREE

The black night rain had made Wythenshawe lonely and sick. Across the estate, the houses were shaken and thrown; they stood where they landed.

The drunk couldn't find the door catch. Amjad had to get out of his seat and help him. Pressed against the edge of the wind, he opened the rear doors and looked down at the sodden body. Amjad forced his voice, hoping to overcome the drift of the wind. The price of the ride was a fiver. The drunk pushed his hand flat into a tight hip pocket. The well-seasoned, screwed note he pulled out had an excremental sheen. Amjad took it and hauled the drunk out. He was glad to shut the door on the back of this damned pissed twat. People talked about dirty money, but what did they mean? The lifeless notes collected in the tills of the cornershops that sold cigarettes in singles and baked beans by the drip? The money taken in curry houses at the business end of the night, overprinted by skid marks after a circuit through the city? Let the Pakis face the embarrassment of paying these soiled tissues into the bank.

When the BMW passed Amjad on the central lines, he didn't decide to follow it. It was taking the road he would have chosen anyway. But when he saw it take a corner, Amjad sped up. He caught sight of it again on the far side of an Escort and allowed another two cars to slip between its tail lights and his Nissan. He could swear to it, this was the same car used in the attack on Jabhar's restaurant. Never mind that he was losing work, Amjad was going to follow the motherfucker. If for no better reason, he might learn something about the monster who had destroyed his friend's dreams. He should know what kind of people didn't care if they started a war between the Blacks and the Pakistanis.

In the language of the holy Koran, Jabhar meant Mighty. In plain English, Jabhar jabbered in shock when he saw the trashed remnants of his restaurant. He had refitted the place himself. Losing the flock wallpaper and the plaster reliefs of Mecca, Jabhar styled his restaurant as a cool blue diner where the light was sharp enough for anyone to see that the modern Moghul food was served on spotless tables. It had been beautiful.

The wiper blades pushed sheets of rainwater across the edge of his bonnet. Beneath the car, the rubber on his retreads created smooth space wherever they failed to grip the road. The BMW was pushing the pace. Perhaps its anti-lock brakes could spin a little friction into the tarmac blacktop – if Amjad ever had to stop, he might slide for miles. On to Princess Park Way, the road lights gave an orange tint to the night but failed against the dense sheets of rain. Amjad had to jump a series of amber lights to keep parity with the BMW, which rode on a lucky green wave through four junctions. Amjad drew square at the fifth set of lights and in that pause, looked over. It was better to look directly. Wiser than being caught stealing a discreet glance.

There was only one man in the BMW. He was, at most, thirty years old and had distinctive tramlines cut into his short hair. Amjad would never have known his name, if his little brother hadn't pointed him out as the Tasmanian.

Amjad put his eyes back on to the road. It was enough. Without better proof, he knew that he'd got the right man. The motherfucker lived in Wythenshaw but drove a

BMW. One day he might be rich enough to afford a house as well as a car. Better, he might end up dead.

The BMW took a right turn. Amjad followed him to the Passenger Club and, when he was sure that was the final stop, Amjad pulled over and turned off his lights. He wasn't sure why he had decided to stay on the tail a little longer. Still, he turned off his radio. At the other end of the wireless link, his uncle would wonder why he had dropped out of the circuit. It would not matter, though.

The No-Smoking sign that did not apply to Amjad was framed by beads. Some of those beads brought good luck – if Amjad knew which ones, he would throw the rest away. He opened a pack of Embassy Filters and lit up. Why would he need luck, if he was only going to sit and watch? All he had to decide was whether he wanted to listen to Bhangra or to a tape of Sufi chants. That did not call for luck.

Over towards the Passenger Club, the Tasmanian got out of his BMW and pointed his key ring at his car. Amjad mouthed the electronic 'beep' that he could not actually hear. In the halogen spotlight above the club door, Amjad saw a flat, squat face and dead eyes. The tramlines in his hair ran all the way around his head, razored into a lightning flash above the nape of his neck. No question, it was the one his little brother had identified as an evil motherfucker. ('Watch your fucking language,' Amjad said when he slapped his brother down. 'Don't let your mum hear you talking that way.')

Although he was not going to do it, Amjad could walk over to the car and look around. He could open it up inside a few minutes. But he could only silence the alarm after he had broken into the car and he did not fancy doing that, not right outside the Passenger Club.

The bouncers, dressed uniformly in black shellsuits, greeted the Tasmanian with hand-slaps. He Yo'ed them back, no smile. He lifted his arms to shoulder height and made a half-turn, forwards and back – but no one actually patted him down. He might be armed now. He might still have the machine guns in his car. Why not? The police had gun-carrying cars travelling endlessly around Manchester, circling the town as aimlessly as lost spirits until they were called to respond. Why wouldn't a gangster do the same? Amjad pulled on his cigarette and sank a little lower in his seat. Driving a Nissan was like carrying a taxi sign on the top of your car, but these streets were worked by unlicensed cabs, driven by black lads who couldn't afford wheels any other way.

Many other people entered the Passenger Club, but at this time the flow was so unhurried that Amjad could look each one over individually and read whatever he could read in their faces. Many were similar to the BMW driver. Most were younger, both males and females but all of them black.

He had been parked for over three-quarters of an hour when he recognised Michael Cross. Striding out from a gallery of concrete pillars under the Moss Side tower blocks, Michael Cross did not shorten his steps for the woman beside him. If he was deliberately forcing the pace, the woman showed no sign of trouble as she kept up with him – despite her heels. It was the same one, the half-caste woman from this afternoon. The one whose mother came from Surinam. What would they do together in the Club? Were they about to dance? Amjad had no idea of the connection between this partly foreign woman and Michael Cross.

When they reached the door, Michael shook hands with the doormen – there was no slapping. When Michael lifted his arms for the security search, they shook their heads as if it was a joke. But one still crunched up the pockets of the jacket he was wearing. As one of the bouncers stood to the side to let Michael pass, Amjad saw him surreptitiously lift the back of Michael's jacket. If he was expecting to find a handgun tucked into the waistband, he didn't find one.

Estela caught the bouncer's clandestine manoeuvre at Michael's back. Did he want a quick sight of Michael's still pert backside? She gave the bouncer a wink, embarrassing him. When it was her turn to be searched, what she did, apart from open her bag, was shrug out of her coat and twirl for the security team. Ain't nothing under this tight dress that should not be there. One of them took her coat for a second and felt down to its pockets. She told them: 'It doesn't matter – it's going in the checkroom anyway.'

All the way down the dark corridor, Michael tried to behave like he didn't know Estela. He was still mad at her. She could cope; she walked ahead of him, smiling freely at anyone who gasped or whistled as she swung past. After she'd checked her coat, she stood waiting for Michael to catch her up. Michael took his time, greeting everyone who greeted him and making it clear he wasn't going to introduce Estela to anyone.

When he reached her at the cloakroom, she tilted her elbow out for him to catch. He slapped it down, he wasn't even going to touch her after what she'd done to him. She followed him through the pair of swing fire-doors and into the club.

Ragga boomed out of a monster sound-system, the walls were sweating in time to the music. Down on the floor, the dancers leant back at impossible angles, thrusting out their hips, hard and low. Their crotches throbbing inside ultra-wide trousers or super-tight skirts. The dancers up-stage led the revolution, their dancing wilder, their clothes more improbable.

She took a few steps, winked at Michael and asked if he wanted anything from the bar.

'Not with you, I'm going club class – upstairs.'

He moved off. She wondered how long he was going to be like this. She had told him, he was the one who first hooked her on martial arts: if he thought about it, it was almost a compliment that she had put him down on his ass.

Like the corridor into the club, the stairs were lined with bodies. It seemed that if anyone wanted to just hang, they chose the main trade routes around the club. The way Michael moved up the stairs, sending out nods rather than full handshakes to anyone who called out to him, it was clear that there was a hierarchy to hanging. Estela frosted her smile. She barely turned her head as the yo-baby-baby brigade tried to distract her. At the head of the stairs, Michael never paused to see if she was still behind him.

She walked into the glare of full light, a smoky bar with airport lounge furniture and pine panelling straight out of the 1970s. Every chair was already taken in the half of the room that Estela could see. Beyond a pine and glass screen, the more secluded half looked as though it might still have sitting room.

Michael said, 'I'll get my own drink. If you're sticking around, don't let on that you're a tranny.'

'I'm not. But if you want to buy – get a gin and French for the lady, Michael.'

The spread of ages in this upstairs bar surprised Estela. Mostly men, some of the older ones could have been sitting in a West Indian social club and not a ragga dance hall. She recognised quite a few, men who weren't so grey the last time she had seen them. Some that she guessed wore grey dreads, underneath the crochet of their caps. The atmosphere was mellow, humming with good-natured laughter, fragrant with grass and rum. Michael returned from the bar with a pint of Guinness held between his finger and thumb, a shot of rum with the remaining fingers. He had nothing at all for her.

When he sank the rum down, he made an mm-mm sound. Delicious. That would show her.

She took short steps between the low-slung, crowded tables, keeping up with Michael as he moved on towards the next set of men he had to greet. A new warmth had soaked into his voice, that could not be pinned on the rum chaser. His handshakes grew longer as he worked his way through the tables. Estela draped a hand across his shoulder, looking round the table she said, 'I'm Estela.'

Everyone turned towards her with interest, and to Michael with approval. Only one of them asked: 'I know you, girl?' Estela told him that he didn't and let him kiss her hand, thinking: you never did that before, Carlton Smith.

She said, 'Can I buy everyone drinks? If someone could help me carry them?'

She got her volunteer. Michael was scowling but all she gave him was a sweet grin. Let him work out if there was a smug edge to it. She passed a fifty over to the man who'd stood to help her. 'The atmosphere's gone straight to my head. Would you mind getting them, honey?'

Michael's friends made room for her around the table. She squeezed in, rolling her eyes and fanning her face; Heavens, I'm such a cissy.

Her eyes were already drifting to the darker half of the bar. She could see that's where the gangstas held court. She was marking them, watching their moves. And she could see the Taz-Man, furthest back in the shadows. He half-turned to accept the hand of his lieutenant. She recognised the gesture – a Hollywood handshake customised for Manchester.

TWENTY-FOUR

Theresa saw Estela first, squashed between ten other people, forced around a single table. They were almost on top of each other in the crowded room, on the overcrowded bench. They seemed to be joking as they passed around a cartoonish joint – the size of a dinghy.

When Estela looked up, she saw Cozy first. She sent him a fresh, wide smile. When she saw Theresa her smile was different, softer and unlascivious.

Estela took extra pains to introduce Theresa around the table but left Michael so far to the last that Michael had to introduce himself, moving in and slipping Theresa a hand that felt gentle, despite the darker callouses on the knuckles.

All Theresa wanted was to manoeuvre Estela to one side, ask her, please if, she could follow her.

In the Ladies, the girls crowded around the mirror but left the stalls free. Theresa pushed Estela through, letting the door swing to when they were both inside. Estela took the seat. Theresa leant against the partition.

Estela said, 'So you found out Burgess is a money launderer.'

How had she known that? She said it was a guess; Theresa wondered how much more she already knew.

'I know he employs morons, so they won' notice how little business passes through the front of the shop.'

'Cozy isn't a moron. This evening, we went down to Burgess's shop and he picked up these.'

Theresa swung the rucksack on to Estela's lap. Estela groaned as the sudden weight fell on her crotch.

'Burgess's accounts with three separate airlines. Cozy says that well over half of Burgess's business is with these companies. And not one of them flies out of Britain.'

Estela pulled open the drawstring on the rucksack and picked out a handful of counterfoils. The airlines were called InterAmericas, Caribair and Fly-East. Theresa asked her if she had heard of any of them. Estela sucked at her lower lip, uncommittedly.

'Cozy said he looked these companies up in a business directory. They're all registered in non-countries, off-shore tax-havens and their sole agent in Britain is John Burgess, through offices in London, Nottingham and Manchester.'

'Where are these flights going?' asked Estela, rustling the wad of counterfoils.

'They just do hops – one strange place to another. A lot are around Indonesian and Malaysian islands. Some of them are internal American flights, or flights around South America and the Caribbean. Burgess sells nearly every seat on each flight, even though Cozy has never seen anyone buying them.'

'So it made him suspicious?'

'It wouldn't have done, he says. He would have just thought that it was good business, that he was too slow to grab or too inexperienced to find. But then a group booking came into the shop, just before Christmas. It was all legitimate, a party of single men going on a luxury outing from their social club or something. Cozy knew they were only going to Miami, for the New Year. But he noticed that Burgess had them booked to fly all over America. They were down for a couple of flights each day. If they had really taken them, they would have spent the whole of their holiday just whizzing from state to state without leaving an airport.'

'How much business of this kind was Burgess doing?'

'Millions, in turnover. Burgess takes a commission on each flight sold.'

'I don' know,' said Estela. She had folded the counterfoils up now and resealed the bag. 'Let someone else work out how he was doing whatever he was doing.'

Theresa said, 'Do you know these companies?'

'Two of them. They're partly owned by men in Colombia and Bolivia. Burgess is laundering cocaine money. The third company, Fly-East, is probably heroin.'

'He's laundering money from both cocaine and heroin?'

'Yes. But perhaps it's all part of the same deal. I heard there are plans to merge some of the different cartels operating on the Pacific rim. Maybe Burgess is helping build a super-cartel.'

'What do we do now?'

'Me? I think I will dance. We can't sit powdering our noses all night.'

Estela slid back the catch, squeezing past Theresa to leave the cubicle. Theresa felt her headache reignite, annoyed that Estela had been so casual. But at least she had taken the bag.

At the washbasin mirror, a girl wriggled to pull her dress straight over her butt. Her friend was at work, teasing the front of her hair into a fan-design. Estela stopped to check on her make-up. Theresa watched her smooth the bow of her upper lip with her finger, re-examine the labial texture, and decide to use her lip-pencil to reassert the desired effect. Theresa twitched impatiently.

'Don' hurry me, Theresa. I'm not a girl any longer, I need time to put right what nature is set on putting wrong.'

Theresa stopped. 'Okay,' she said. 'I'll wait outside.'

In the lounge bar, Michael Cross still had the same seat, half-turned, talking to a man he called Uncle. Not really talking, it was more that he was nodding. Cozy was standing apart from the group. He was looking around, managing not to look awkward but failing to look at ease.

Theresa looked at him. 'Who are you waiting for?'

His eyes sailed past Theresa's face. 'The glamour puss is back. What are we getting involved in?'

Estela was out of the toilets. She had worked the shoulders of her dress lower so the material now hung from the top of her arms and stretched tight over her bosoms. Somehow, she had persuaded each breast to poke a little higher out of the top of the dress. Cozy was not the only one to have noticed her. As she came back through the lounge bar, she was swinging her hips in a preposterous burlesque.

'What is she up to?' asked Cozy.

Theresa didn't know. She watched the long pendulum of Estela's torso navigate around the heads of the seated drinkers. Was this a Latin move, a solo salsa or lambada? She looked like a stripper. When she came to a halt, her hips were slung at forty-five degrees and her arse sticking out like a mantlepiece. Theresa looked around the table to see what kind of reaction she had provoked. Nearly everyone's eyes were on Estela. Only Michael Cross reacted differently. Theresa believed she saw her headache flit across the table and hit Michael between the eyes. He flickered in pain.

Estela inclined towards the table. Tilting slightly at the waist, she was playing her bosom to the gallery, rotating her balconette across all the seated heads.

'Anyone care to dance?'

Theresa pulled Cozy's elbow: 'Come on, I've had enough

of this. I've got to go somewhere – and you'd better drive me.'

Estela saw Theresa and Cozy leave, but only from the corner of her eye. A quiet commotion to the rear distracted her. The Taz-Man came spooling out of the shadows. Two taller boys trailed at his shoulder.

'Hey. We together again.'

Estela passed him a zero-shaped smile, a modellish pout. Everyone looked from Estela to the contender.

The Taz-Man gave Estela two hands, both huge. When Estela slipped her hand between them, he held on to it tightly – he did not look as though he was going to let her slip out in a hurry.

'Estela, I wanted to ask, what kind of name's that?'

'A star's name, honey. What kind of name is Taz-Man?'

'Short for Dee-Evil Taz-Man. First name Dee, second name Evil, last name The Taz-Man.'

'First name Estela, last name Santos.' Estela had made no move to release her hand.

TWENTY-FIVE

Amjad felt the rain made him invisible, like he were unseen, all-seeing, half in his body and half in the air. He continued to watch the door of the Passenger Club and he continued to have no idea why he was doing it. He had turned off the tape of Sufi chants. They had worked too well, managing to both relax him and thrill him with desire. What he needed, now, was to empty himself while keeping himself on edge. He tuned his radio to the local news.

It was blowing hard tonight. In the tiny gap between the top of the door and the window, through the space that he'd left to stop his breath clouding the inside of his cab, the wind blew spits of freezing drizzle. How many degrees just above zero was Manchester tonight? Amjad lit another cigarette. If he'd known he wouldn't be working again this evening, would he have brought himself a quarter-bottle of whiskey? Or would he have carried on with his no-drinking regime? Muslims should not drink, because they end up acting stupid when they do. That's what he'd decided, seeing his cousin Iqbal crying over a dumb Indian film. He'd told him, make some black coffee. Turn off that Hindi crap and put on a Jackie Chan video – stop acting like a fucking wanker.

On the other hand, in this pissing weather, he should do what the Brits did. Drink whiskey because whiskey works like an eighteen-tog duvet in pissy Manchester rainstorms. It was like looking into a wiggly mirror, trying to see through the night rain. Hardly anyone had entered the Passenger Club in the last hour and he was up past one o'clock without being paid for it. He saw a couple leaving the club, that was it. Strange that they were white; he had thought the Passenger Club was getting a bit heavy for the white kids. They crossed over the paved front and passed in front of his Nissan – a dark-haired girl hurrying ahead of a long-haired boy. They walked over to a yellow Marina he hadn't even noticed before. That was strange, too. He had heard the TV people describe the car involved in the shooting that afternoon as a charcoal-grey BMW. He knew it was a yellow Marina because his nephew Mohammed Amir had seen everything. It had been better than Jackie Chan, Mohammed had said. The back doors flew open and this ugly fucker, with a pony tail, kind of cartwheeled out of the back. He took a Smith and Wesson off this black lad and came up shooting. If Mohammed had had his camcorder with him, he would have sent it to Hong Kong. Give some of those directors a few ideas for top action sequences, no messing.

When the couple had driven out of sight, Amjad returned to his stake-out. The bouncers were still at the door, keeping out from the rain. Amjad watched them stamp their feet and blow on cupped hands. He bet they wished they were wearing more than shellsuits. The bouncers over at the Gravity wore Crombies. That was more like it, more the style for standing around past one in this weather. Mohammed Amir said the Lexus was driven by the head man over at the Gravity. The one who walked liked a body-builder but was built like a brickie, a beer-gut on him like a bin-liner filled with water. That was one thing the TV people had got right: they said that the security team from the Gravity were involved in the incident. The story was repeated on the local radio news before the announcer turned to a new story: a group of

New Yorkers, visiting from the Bronx, had decided to leave their flat in Whalley Range. They said that they found the area too violent, they had all been mugged too many times. The radio played a snatch of a taped interview. Amjad didn't know what a Ho was, but the New Yorkers seemed to have a problem with that, too.

There was another couple leaving the club now. This was what he'd been waiting for – the Tasmanian. He hadn't expected to see him with the Latin woman. Now she was tied up with this bad motherfucker, Amjad did not know what to think. He could see that she had her arm looped through his as they came out of the door. She had withdrawn it by the time they got to the pavement, but only so that she could hold her coat above her head and keep her hair from getting wet. Amjad would have said she was too classy for a shit-eating smack dealer.

The man's BMW was parked right out front of the club, in a position of honour. The classy Latin let the gangster walk ahead of her to the car, holding his car keys in front of him like Captain Kirk holding his Fazer. He scooted around to the front and once he was inside the car, the woman started towards it and opened the passenger-side door. Amjad could see the man had turned towards her side of the car. When she was in, he leant over. Amjad guessed that they were snogging – what the fuck was this about? Now she had pulled away from him again, he was nodding. Turning to the front, he put his hands on the wheel. Amjad saw the headlights come on. They were going to move off.

Amjad started his own car, but left his own headlights off. He had to think. If he just pulled out behind the BMW, he would be too obvious. If he followed them with his headlamps off, the bouncers at the Passenger Club would notice and guess what he was doing. If he turned the lights on, then the Latin and her lover would see him.

He threw the Nissan into reverse as he started its engine. He decided to back around the corner to his rear. Then he could pull out with his headlamps on, as though he was coming from around the corner. He would probably pass by the BMW before it had started, but that was good. No one would guess that he was tailing them if he was ahead of their car. There was only one direction they could go, unless they wanted to head into a dead end. Amjad knew he could slip back on to their tail when he reached the dual carriageway.

As he crossed in front of the headlight beam of the BMW, Amjad kept his eyes to the front. He didn't want to risk stealing a glance. He tried to keep his speed moderately slow so that he didn't end up too far ahead of their car. He had his eyes on his rearview mirror as the BMW pulled out from the road by the Passenger Club. He saw it turn in completely the wrong direction, showing him its red tail-lights as it headed into the maze of dead ends beneath the prefab hulks of Moss Side. Shit. Amjad resisted the urge to throw a u-ee or a handbrake turn. He would have to play it cool. Find a place to turn around naturally and then follow every road until he found them again. What were they doing, trying to lose themselves in the undercroft of Moss Side? She couldn't intend to give that motherfucker a gobble.

The Taz-Man's BMW was sunk in the shadows of the undercroft. He stretched a hand over to cup Estela's belly then dragged it across the ruffled material of her tight dress until he had hold of her right breast. Estela bent towards him. His skin breathed with the leathery scent of Fendi aftershave; the open pores on his cheeks grew wider as she drew herself on to his lips. His tongue flipped into her mouth, pushing forward as a kind of foretaste, and retreated. She cupped the hard flatpack of his breast in her hand. He was a bull of a man, short but meatily solid. His tits felt like a weightlifter's; his nipples prodded at his T-shirt. She got the teat between her thumb and forefinger and gave a long slow tug downwards. She felt a wave run through his body until, where their hips touched, the spasm hit his crotch and ended in a short involuntary writhe. Estela dropped her hand into the space between his legs. His cock had begun to unfurl inside his over-sized jeans, she felt it tense, relax and grow against the back of her fingers. She wriggled against the leather seat of the BMW and settled on a better position. From here, she could press her palm against his cock and begin to massage it through the black denim.

'Baby wants to ride that Mother? I tell you, I'm gonna do you a big favour.'

When did the American strain seep into his Mancunian accent? It had begun the moment he got hot. Even as they were walking out of the Passenger Club, it was 'Mother' this, 'Mother' that, in a hybrid dialect – it wasn't exactly fake, it happened only as he began to lose his judgement and control. It happened as she stroked around the curves of his tight black ass while they waited for the cloakroom girl to fetch her coat. Estela couldn't say it was unattractive.

'You want this mo', baby. I tell you, it's sweet as you – you gonna get along with it fine.'

She pulled at the top edge of his flies, the buttons popped in sequence all the way down to the crotch. Estela slipped her hand inside and reached the base of his cock, at the point where it had slipped out from the front of his shorts. She hooked a finger underneath it and drew it out from his trousers. Half-hard, it lay like a question-mark against his lap. She partially covered it with her hand and looked up to his eyes. He had them open. They were kind of piggy. The scar tissue that had built up around his brows made his eyes appear to recede. Traces of acne lay on his cheeks like black maggots. She should have kept her eyes on his dick – that looked as though it could be a thing of beauty, a joyous foreskinner. The Taz-Man was ugly in the face but there was a grace to his body that pumping iron hadn't completely erased. Estela chose to look him in the face because that was a part of her technique. She got him to focus on her eyes.

'I want to suck you, sugar. I want you in my mouth.'

He mumbled unintelligibly but with commitment. Estela had him hooked. She kept her eyes turned up towards his as she went down on his cock. If the position inside the car was less cramped, she would have kept her eyes on his throughout. Big puppy-dog eyes turned up in special pleading with his cock half-way down her throat, that turned hetero men inside out with emotions they could not handle. She opened wide and took all his dick in her mouth, easing outwards as it shrugged off the last traces of flaccidity.

'Stay with it, sugar, stay with it,' he said.

She pulled back her teeth, cushioning their sharper edges with the flesh of her lips. She pumped, up and down. His cock was fully hard, fully eight inches long – she estimated. It felt to have more than an inch over the average. The Taz-Man's right hand was cupping the back of her head, but he was not pressing down. She forced herself to surge forward. The helmet tipped against the back of her throat and nosed through. Estela drew back before she quite gagged and controlled the flood of saliva. With the next push, her mouth was full of spit but his dick was fully lubricated. He could fuck her in the face; she had her throat open wide enough for a sword-swallowing trick.

He was panting hard, but trying to keep his crotch still. She had him, he had already given in. He was trying to keep her as shallow as possible, trying to rein her back from the depths. He had only ever had it licked before, she could tell. He had never fucked a throat. She pulled upwards, fixing him a soaking and crooked smile that dripped with saliva.

'I don' believe I'm so hot and wet. You'll fuck me hard, won' you, Sugar-Devil?'

The Taz-Man nodded, uh-huh. He was still trying to control it, breathing with an exaggeratedly slow rhythm. Yeah, I'll fuck you.

Estela felt for the mechanism that would collapse her whole seat backwards. Taz-Man had half-turned and lifted himself up. He had one knee bent on the driving seat, the other leg straight out under the wheel. He was trying to wriggle out of his jeans. His cock swung outwards with its own inertia – it had a rare curve to it, standing upright before curving downwards. It was distinctly thicker in the middle than at the ends; it looked like a leaping porpoise wearing a saddle.

'I'm so ready for you, sugar,' she said.

Lying almost flat on her seat, she was getting her legs as wide apart as possible. With her hands in her crotch, she ripped at the press-studs that secured the bottom of her lycra body-stocking. His ears seemed to be cocked to the sound each stud made as it burst. He had his pants to his knees, now. He began to manoeuvre himself between her legs.

'I am so ready. I wan' to give you the biggest surprise,' she said.

He heard the velcro rip – perhaps he thought it was another layer of clothing. Estela pulled the Luger out as the velcro bands holding it in place slipped away.

'Look,' said Estela. 'It's as big as your cock.'

She held the Luger with two hands. Pointing upwards into the Taz-Man's face, for a moment it mirrored the angle of his drooping cock. Then the cock withered and shrank, just like the Taz-Man. He collapsed into his driver's seat. Estela swung her legs to the side, off the dashboard, and tucked them to one side. Now that she'd got her breath back . . .

Her voice came out in a hard Manchester drawl, 'It looks like you're out of fucking business.'

His tail between his legs, he still had just enough testosterone dribbling around his body to ask her what she wanted.

'The whole fucking show—we want all of Manchester.'

Amjad pulled around the dumpsters and saw the driver's seat door swing open. The gangster came out naked butt first. When he was fully out, and had edged backwards a good four yards from the car, the woman followed. She was feet first, relaxedly elegant as she brought her legs together and straightened out of the car. She wiggled the gun towards the trunk of his car. The man hobbled that way, trying to pull his trousers up as he went. Amjad saw the woman turn swiftly and pull the keys out of the ignition switch. She never let her gun leave the man.

She made him lie flat on his face, by the side of the car, as she opened the trunk. Amjad decided to make his move. He drove slowly towards her. As she heard him, she turned. The gun remained on the man, but now she had a new gun in her other hand. She must have picked this second gun out of the trunk of the gangster's car. She was pointing it straight at Amjad.

'It's okay, it's me.' Amjad had to sit up in his seat and speak out of the open crack at the top of his window. He hurriedly wiped condensation off the inside of the glass and smiled at the woman.

'Estela, isn't it? Estela. Remember me?' He thought he'd better not actually say his name. The gangster on the ground had not yet looked around – Amjad preferred not to be recognised. Unless this woman was intending to shoot the motherfucker.

'Oh, hello.' Estela tucked her newest gun under her arm and pulled open the back door of Amjad's Nissan.

She threw this new gun in first. It was followed by another few weapons, all quite big. Then a green Adidas bag.

'Let's go,' she said as she walked around to the passenger seat door. Just as she was opening it, she fired down at the ground. The big handgun jerked up. Amjad couldn't tell if she had shot him. Driving away, he tried to get a glimpse in his side-view mirror. The figure on the ground had his hands clasped behind his head. Amjad was sure that he could see him shaking. She hadn't killed him, after all.

TWENTY-SIX

They recognised her immediately. The desk sergeant looked up at her and called over to a constable: the dark lady had arrived. Theresa set her mouth in a line and nodded hello.

'I heard that you want to see me.'

'Call off the APB, lads. Public Enemy Number One's just turned herself in,' said the desk sergeant to the crowd of young constables who were leering at Theresa around an open door.

One constable handed a xeroxed photo to Theresa; it was her face, taken from the security video. He asked her if she would autograph it for him. She couldn't believe it. It was like the first day at school – all the older boys had come out to see if she lived up to her reputation.

'We were all wondering, were you as gorgeous as you looked on the video.'

'Too right she is, sarge.'

As she was shown down a corridor, another constable cooed from a side office: 'I'll wait for you, love. No matter how long you get.'

'If you'd like to take a seat here,' said the sergeant. 'We won't keep you long, Miss O'Donnell.'

They had already found out her name. Well, that was police work. Theresa guessed that her mam had probably phoned in, after seeing her picture on the news. She took a seat on a naugahyde-covered bench and looked at the peculiar, pinhead photofits on the walls. A couple of constables hung around by the door, asking if she would like coffee. A cigarette? Food? A date? Theresa began to feel confident that she could see the process through to the end. She knew her story would convince all the policemen she had met so far. Although these stiff, blushing post-teen police would not be the ones interviewing her. She turned to the two young coppers at the door and forced out a smile – yeah, okay, a coffee would be nice. It would keep her awake, yeah. Although she hoped she wouldn't be here long.

'I hope you are. Don't take that the wrong way.'

'If you want driving home, ask for me, all right?'

But when she asked them if they knew why she was there, and it was clear that neither of them knew, her spirits slid like yesterday's mascara.

'What does helping-with-enquiries mean?'

They shrugged amongst themselves. It could mean anything. Great. Just great. It looked as though she would be here for the rest of the night. When Cozy left her on the pavement, just out of sight of the station at Old Trafford, Theresa had told him not to wait, although he had offered. The story was fixed, she was determined to take it straight round to the police. But she'd had to stop and re-collect her breathing before she entered the lobby.

The station reverberated with the muffled tap of police issue Doctor Martens. The corridors above and around her hummed with the insect-life of soldier ants, the soft hexapody of men and women marching from coffee machines to desks, from the xerox to the IBM. Theresa was squeezed between the plastic flooring tiles and the artifical ceilings, condensed by the strip lighting. She imagined a termite hill, injected with anti-freeze so that its maze of tunnels glowed fluorescent blue.

DI Green's dull flat-foot step cut across every other rhythm. Theresa had only heard DI Green before. Despite him wearing the regulation shoes of the more junior policemen, Theresa recognised his approach from ten yards. She waited to match her impressions with a face. All she thought: he's bald – or there's a degree of balding. When he spoke, his image flicked into focus. Granite-grey face and watery eyes. The crooked swerve of his lower teeth was emphasised by nicotine stains that framed each separate tooth. Theresa fixed on the teeth as he thanked her for coming.

'We're all hoping that what you have to say clinches this business for us. If you'll follow me, we can get cracking.'

Theresa paused while DI Green peeled the two young policemen off the doorframe, then passed through to the corridor. As they climbed the station stairs together, DI Green explained that they had a clear idea of the relevant events. He told her that they had built a kind of scaffolding, an hypothetical matrix.

'There's established procedures for everything in police-work, except what I do. I've got to make it up fresh, each and every time. This one's a cunt, I tell you. I've got a series of tangential incidents but nothing that really gives me the full picture. I can put all the separate bits together, but I'm still left with a whacking great hole. And that's all I've got. A hole that wants stuffing.'

DI Green spoke deliberately. Theresa didn't look at him as they climbed the stairs, she would have long enough to look at him once their interview began. But she did listen. She caught the change in register as he finished his procedural description. She knew he was smiling as he watched for her reaction but she wasn't yet petrified – she was only playing dumb.

'Have you ever seen anyone pouring concrete?' DI Green waited for her to answer. 'No? . . . What they do, they make a wooden frame, then they pour the concrete inside the frame. When it's dry, they smash the wood away. You see the parallel? I've built something that looks solid but it's not what I want. It's only an outline. What I hope you'll do, is fill in the spaces so that when I pour in the concrete and knock my scaffolding away I'm left with this perfectly formed solution.'

'And I'm six feet under a ton of concrete.'

'That's right. You're not stupid are you? Don't try acting it when we get to the interview room – or you're fucked, Miss O'Donnell.'

In the interview room, he sat her down and told her that he'd have to leave her alone again for a minute. He needed to have a second bobby present, so that she could be sure everything was above board. She had time to look around, to notice the TV that was stood on a wheeled pedestal. She had time to squirm in the plastic seat and realise she wasn't ever going to get comfortable. When DI Green returned with a junior partner, she saw that he had the video tape in the pocket of his once-blue jacket.

It was DI Green's junior who spoke first. 'Ms O'Donnell. Would you be surprised to hear you were filmed by security standing over the body of John Caxton?'

'No. I think I must have been the first one to reach him, after he was shot.'

'Why didn't you come forward earlier?' Junior said.

'I might have been the next one shot. I was scared.'

DI Green kept her under his gaze. Theresa was only aware of him out of the side of her eyes as she talked to the younger man. She knew that he hadn't moved. When he did, she had to switch back to him.

'Scared? Why was that? What did you have to be scared about?'

'Of Mr Burgess?' asked Junior.

'No. I was scared of the Colombian woman.'

'Why were you scared of her?' DI Green, again.

'She shot Yen.'

There was a pause, Theresa didn't know how to read it. She waited for DI Green to speak again.

'You saw a woman you describe as being Colombian shoot John Caxton?'

'I didn't see her shoot him. But I saw her with the gun, later, when she tried to kill me. So she must have shot Yen.'

'This woman attempted to shoot you?'

'Yes. After I saw Yen and I ran out of Junk's room, she was coming towards me with a gun.'

Junior looked over to DI Green. They decided to take it more slowly. Junior just asked his superior frankly: 'What shall we get? The whole story for the night?' DI Green turned back to Theresa.

'Why do you say she's Colombian?'

'She told Yen where she was from. He told me, after. He had met her the night before. She picked him up in a bar, the WARP. She bought him drinks all night and then took him back to her place. Yen said she also asked him all kinds of stuff. In the end, she made him so nervous that he did one. He ran out on her while she was sleeping.'

'He waited until she was asleep, then left. Why was he nervous?'

'She asked him all kinds of stuff about where he worked, about the way Burgess runs his travel agents. He didn't tell her anything. Yen was too sharp. He knew what Burgess was doing. He knew about all the fake receipts and the amount of money pouring into the shop from God knows where. And once she said she was Colombian – he began to think 'cocaine'. Yen always said that Burgess was a monster for coke. He had this idea that Burgess must be laundering money for some big-time cocaine dealers.'

'John Caxton told you all of this? That Burgess is a coke addict who launders drug money, and that a woman picked him up in a bar so that she could pump him for information on behalf of Colombian cocaine barons?'

'No. He didn't say it like that. At first, he thought she was just chatting because she fancied him. But the questions became more specific. It was obvious that she was interested in a stack of counterfoils for dodgy sales that had gone missing from Burgess's shop. He said she was quite subtle, but it was clear that that was what she wanted to know. He kept quiet.'

'What had happened to these counterfoils?'

'Yen had them. Yen always came across as stupid, but he wasn't. He knew there was something weird about Burgess's business and he took the counterfoils so that he'd have proof. He showed them to me.'

'When was that?'

'Yesterday.'

'Yesterday? You mean Friday?'

What day was it today? Theresa knew that she had to be precise: 'The day he died. Just before he died. That woman killed him and when I got to him, the counterfoils were gone.' Theresa stopped. She remembered Yen's death face.

In the following silence, DI Green began drumming his fingers across the formica tabletop. He started making a staccato mm-mm sound out of pursed lips. As he snapped back to earth, he slapped his palms flat on the table: 'Right. Take us through last night.'

Again? 'From the beginning, when we arrived with Junk? . . . Okay. Junk left me and Yen in his room. He had to go downstairs and keep Burgess company. Burgess claimed he was a social coke-head, he didn't like to snort alone. While Junk was away, Yen rolled a joint. We sat smoking it, just chilling. I started teasing him about this older woman who had picked him up in the WARP. That's when he showed me the counterfoils, and told me about all the questions this Colombian woman asked him.

'Later on, I left him and went for a wander around. I'm not sure how long I was gone. When I came back up the stairs, Yen was lying there. I shut the door quick so no one could see. If anyone passes out at the Gravity, they call an ambulance and you end up on the local news. I didn't know he was dead, I just thought it was . . .' she paused, 'Something else, you know.'

'Drugs?'

'Yes, I thought he might have o-deed. He had taken some pills and he didn't know what the fuck they were. And then he'd passed out. I tried to check him over. I mean, I went to check him over. But when I got close, I saw he'd been stabbed, or something. I didn't know he'd been shot. All I saw was a hole and a lot of blood. I looked for the counterfoils. They were gone. Then I ran.

'The first person I saw, was this same Colombian woman running back towards me, throwing open the doors to the lighting room and the DJ's box as she came down the corridor. When she saw me, I screamed. I was sure she was the one who'd killed Yen, I don't know why. I saw her go into a pocket, and I caught sight of her gun. I lunged at her, pushed her off-balance and ran away. All I wanted to do was get out of the club as quickly as possible.'

Junior turned to ask DI Green if they should look at the video again. DI Green reached down and brought out the video tape: 'You put it in the machine.'

Theresa had remembered the whole sequence. Her version worked – she only had to repeat elements of her story at the right moment in the tape. She didn't have to change a word.

At the moment she collided with Estela, Junk reached

Estela's shoulder. He seemed to stop her from falling but as he caught her, he staggered. Estela was propelled sideways and into the room where Yen's body lay. The video showed there was no real escape for her. Junk seemed to scream, or make some kind of noise, and suddenly a crowd had formed. Estela was trapped with Yen's body.

TWENTY-SEVEN

Letting himself through a side door at the Gravity, Junk heard the voices of Bernard and Burgess below him. This side entrance opened on to a stairwell. If Junk continued down the steps, he would find himself in Burgess's office, in the cellar below. He didn't think that the pleasantries they might exchange, if he hobbled in on them, would be worth the trip. Instead, he stood on the ground floor landing and listened. He couldn't make out the details of their conversation but it seemed that Bernard had only just arrived – perhaps only minutes before Junk. As he limped towards the Gravity, Junk had kept his eye open for both Bernard's and Burgess's cars. He had only found one, a Lexus LS400: its engine still warm enough to condense the drizzle above its bonnet. Because he had found no signs of ballistic damage, Junk guessed that it was Burgess's. Bernard and Burgess drove identical cars. Junk had placed one frozen palm on the hood, hoping to feed off the heat.

He hadn't prepared for the consistent deterioration of the weather when he repacked his bag. Now, with his multiple non-fatal injuries, the weather was beginning to bear down on him. He shouldered the satchel that he had stuffed with his remaining tapes with difficulty.

Junk checked the latch on the external door. Now that he was sure that he hadn't been heard, he tiptoed weakly down the landing and entered the main area of the club. The place should have been rammed, tonight being a Saturday. An empty nightclub always provoked strange emotions in Junk. He sensed the after-image of all the energy dissipated here, the ghostly negative of the elements that would charge the atmosphere on a good night. The police had not allowed the club to open – they insisted that it remain shut for forensic reasons. Would Burgess have argued, when he was told? Would he instruct his lawyer to demand that the place be run as usual – that the cops were infringing his right to trade? Junk could imagine Burgess doing that; arguing. 'So what – one cunt died, two thousand other punters didn't.'

For sure, Burgess would have argued in the old days. Now that he worked to make his interests appear respectable, he would probably have rolled over. Let the club stay shut: let them believe that we did it out of respect for the memory of the dead boy. There was a chill in the club tonight. Was that a part of Yen's dead memory? There was no one who had raved, danced, drugged like Yen. There were times when Yen single-handedly created all the atmosphere the Gravity needed. Junk would watch him from above, looking through the window of his little cabin in the sky. He would see Yen standing on a pedestal, in the centre of the dance floor, so far out of it – so totally on one – that he lifted the whole rhythm and tempo. The DJ would have to hunt for records with more intense b.p.m.s, finding himself wrong-footed by the sudden explosion of energy.

Junk walked across the stage and dropped down to the empty dance floor. As still as this, the club looked exactly like the thing it was: an old warehouse. Junk limped through sombre space where the only undead element was the echo. When the Gravity was full, the crush of bodies acted as a physical barrier to the soundwaves. When Burgess first bought the warehouse and had it refitted as a club, Junk watched the sound engineers with interest as they calculated by what amount the number of punters would absorb and kill the sound. It wasn't simply a question of turning the volume up so loud that the level of amplification cancelled out the effect of the mass of the crowd. These engineers – they described themselves as sonic architects – had to find ways of bouncing the sound around the club. They hung specially constructed sheets from the ceiling, explaining that they would reflect sound and redirect it back into the heart of the club. Even after the Gravity's grand opening night, they were still running around – checking for pockets of dead space where no sound could penetrate.

With the place empty, every one of Junk's footsteps reverberated through the club. He tried to keep to the balls of his feet. He was sure no sound would penetrate through the concrete floor to the cellars. Still, he tried to walk with as much stealth as his injuries allowed. He clasped the satchel of tapes in front of him, and began the climb up to the balcony and his cabin beyond. The steel mesh floor of the balcony made a different sound, a soft ringing that filled the club. Junk knew this noise, too, could never reach Burgess and Bernard in the cellar below. He enjoyed the fact of sound, as much as the concretion of light. He liked that space could never be empty, that solar and sonic forces created fields of qualitatively less dense and more dense matter. He pushed through the molecular aggregations and waviform curtains that supported him and pressed forward to his private cabin at the balcony end.

The police had signed their arrival and departure with blue-and-white plastic ribbons. Junk's cabin had a criss-cross of police incident tape barring the door. Junk ignored it. He pulled it down with his free hand and swung his bag through the door with the other. He was here to entertain himself. From the few videos at his disposal, he could choose anything and watch it in silence.

He could watch and wait or do whatever he felt like until the time was right. Fingering through the breast pocket on his jacket, he found the wrap. His chief priority was to maintain his edge. It was a pledge, a duty. Junk unfolded the paper into a flat diamond. Inside the amphetamine crystals were neatly packed into a powdery slab. Under the anglepoise light, the dusty crystals glittered with a blueish whiteness that Junk liked. He stuck the edge of his yale key into the powder and brought a fat globule up to his nose, his sinuses were already snapping and buzzing.

Junk staggered as he crossed the balcony. He had his bag strapped to his shoulder, dangling at his back. His hands were free to carry the crate of tonic water bottles that he'd found beneath the counter of the cocktail bar. As he manhandled the crate forward along the steel gantry floor, the video screens above his head played out scenes of molecular reality – disintegration, debruised particles in high-speed expansion, warped matter. Junk had reconfigured every myth of modern physics on his editing desk, using snippets of kung fu videos, disaster movies and snow boarding sequences. The tower block never collapses after the force of an explosion, it continues hurtling forward, creating new axes of energy displacement as it speeds across white space. The screens above the dance floor absorbed every image that Junk projected against them. Never think of a screen as flat; it's a wave of quantum matter waiting to be surfed. Against the resonant silence, Junk's heavy-footed limp struck dull notes off the steel mesh floor. Sound is only sluggish light – Junk's video tapes bounced off every surface, re-animating the Gravity, passing through Junk as though he were already unsolid. His bruises, the cracked rib he'd only lately discovered, responded to the higher and lower ranges of the spectrum: the infra- and ultra-rays that he wished he could see as well as he could feel. Junk was cranked up, geared for the moment. Still, he took a rest when he reached the balcony edge, stopping to balance the crate on the edge of the nearest table. When he was ready, Junk lifted the crate past his shoulder and up over the balustrade.

The crate hit the dance floor below. Trampolining off the wood, the bottles that did not smash with the first impact bounced higher than the crate. As the crate hit the floorboards a second time, the glass blew out in froth and shards. The foaming tonic water held the explosion in a bubbling cloud, punctured by fragments of spinning debris. The huge sound decompounded in layers: the initial impact; the collision of crate, glass and wood; the echoes; the aftershocks; the returning echo. Beneath the floorboards, disturbed in his offices, Burgess must be staring upwards and asking, 'What the fuck?' If he caught Bernard's eye, what would he register: shock, fear, confusion? Paranoia, sclerosis, sonic dyslexia? Junk waited to hear their feet on the cellar steps. He wanted to be ready, before they passed into view.

He watched them come running across the stage area, stopping themselves at the edge when they saw the remains of the crate. They looked to each other to explain the scene and the damage; the video images that free-wheeled across the expanse of the club, the broken and scattered glimmers of glass and plastic. Blinking against the uncertain light, they turned their faces upwards and scoured the outer limits of the club. Junk had fallen back to the shadows, he needed time to unpack his bag.

'Who's that?' Burgess shouted.

Junk took a beat's pause before answering, making sure that he was hidden before he emptied his bag on to the nearest table: 'It's me. Junk.'

'Junk? What the fuck are you doing?'

Bernard dropped from the stage to the dance floor. Junk stopped him there: 'Hold it. You're not coming up.'

Bernard stopped and looked up again, trying to pinpoint Junk before he turned back to Burgess: 'Do you think the bastard's armed?'

'I don't know.' Burgess raised his voice: 'Hey, Junk, have you still got that gun?'

Bernard had pulled his hand clear of the pocket of his coat. He did have a gun. Junk could see the chrome finish on a flattish handgun.

'Hey, Junk. Wait there, I'll be back,' said Burgess. He returned up-stage and disappeared through the rear door into the stairwell. Bernard remained, keeping talking, hoping that Junk would betray himself. He kept his piglet eyes fixed on the balcony.

'You made a right fucking mess of my car, John Quay. I don't dare to think about the fucking repair bill. And some of my boys are a bit shaken up. Know what I mean? A bit fucking nervy.'

Junk kept to the shadows. The packages that he had taken out of his shoulder bag were ready on the table in front of him. Two packages: one large-ish, the size of a kilo sugar pack; one small enough to fit inside an envelope.

'Are you still there, John Quay? Speak up. I want to know what you are going to do about my car.'

Junk kept his mouth buttoned, but he was still there. He felt as though he was all there. He bristled with energy, his pulse ran in time with images on the video screen. By the time Burgess reappeared carrying a gun, Junk was all set. He stared patiently down to the stage where Bernard and Burgess stood, but at a molecular level he was speeding.

He had no idea what kind of gun Burgess was carrying.

It looked like a scuba diver's harpoon gun. It could have been a standard handgun, fitted with an incredibly long barrel or perhaps a shotgun that had been customised with the handgrip and trigger of a pistol. Burgess held it with one hand on the grip and the other half-way along the barrel. As Burgess racked it, Junk realised that it was an elaborate pump-action shotgun.

'We thought we'd better get some firepower,' said Burgess. 'Now that Paul Sorel has been reborn as a killer tart and you've regressed to your gun-toting vigilante stage, I thought we should walk prepared.'

Junk's eyes flickered over the video screens. His tape was still running; a beautiful segue from a monster truck derby to Vietnamese fighting crickets. The smaller one was waving its feelers in excitement, as it took the other into a death-grip. Junk reached into the larger pack and sprinkled a handful of white powder across his face, blessing himself as he soaked it up. He wanted a ceremonial flourish to the storyboard. He needed to ritualise this coming scene.

'What about Paul Sorel?' Burgess waved his shotgun. 'What's the crack with him?'

They were moving forwards. Bernard, passing over the dance floor to his right, was making for the steps. Junk ran his palm over his outstretched tongue and licked away the last of the powder. He was ready.

'I said, hold it.' Junk shouted. 'You're not coming up.'

Bernard crouched slightly, now. He had his gun pointing up towards the balcony. Burgess crossed over to a pillar and took cover behind it.

'Just tell us, Junk. Are you armed or not?' Burgess asked.

'No.'

Burgess reappeared, visibly relaxed. He signalled over

to Bernard, waving him towards the balcony stairs again. Junk shouted at them to stop.

'Stay where you are. I've got something to tell you, Burgess. If you shoot me, you won't hear it. If you come up here, I'll throw myself off the balcony.'

Burgess waved over to Bernard, stopping him: 'Okay, what do you have to tell me, Junk?'

'Wait. I'm coming to the edge of the balcony.'

Junk walked into the light, they could see him now. He skimmed the smaller package over the edge of the balcony and watched it sail end-over-end towards the dance floor.

'What's that,' asked Burgess. 'A ransom demand?'

'No, it's yours. It's the last of the coke you sent me to buy. I've come to hand in my resignation, I won't be running errands for you any more.'

'You're resigning? Yeah? . . . You're fucking fired, you twat,' said Burgess as he dropped on to the dance floor. He walked over to the envelope and picked it up. 'Nice thought, though. Offering me a golden handshake. What do they say: up in smoke or up your nose. Pound for pound, it costs more than gold. Don't do it, doo be doo be doo.'

Burgess unwrapped his cocaine: 'You've not spiked this with Ajax scouring powder, have you, Junk?'

Burgess licked his finger and dug the wettened tip into the coke. He examined the dust that stuck to it. He must have approved of whatever he saw. He rubbed his hands together, charged with anticipation.

'What, there must be four, five grammes here, Junk.'

'Six. I was ripping you off, these past years. I gave you a good deal this once, for old time's sake,' said Junk.

'Nice gesture, coming up honest at the end. A bit bloody late, though.' Burgess paused; holding his gun and the envelope in one hand, he felt through his pockets with the other. 'Hey, Bernie. Have you got a tenner I could borrow?'

Bernard recrossed towards Burgess, holding out a ten-pound note. Burgess nodded his thanks as he took the note and the envelope over to the edge of the stage. He laid down his gun and took out a credit card. Once he'd opened the envelope and scraped part of the powder on to the stage, he chopped through the pile with the edge of his credit card to break down the larger crystals. Seeming satisfied with the grain quality, he formed it into a line and rolled up the note.

'Hey, Junk,' he shouted over his shoulder. Conspiratorially, was that it? Sartorially? 'I never asked you, what do you think of the theory that drugs kill you?'

'I never thought about it,' said Junk.

'You're still alive – kind of.'

'Yeah, I'm still alive,' said Junk.

'And you did a shit load of amphetamine. Which is pretty toxic stuff, even though I made it myself. Not too good for nasal membranes, tooth enamel, your liver. How's your liver? . . . Cocaine should be better for you, considering it's a natural product. On the other hand, it goes through so much treatment with hydrochloric acid – it's probably just as noxious as speed. It would probably burn the roof off your fucking head if it didn't have anaesthetic properties. What do you reckon?'

'I wouldn't know. I don't know anything about cocaine,' said Junk.

'No, I remember. You're too low-rent for coke, you just run out and buy it for me. What kind of drugs do the scum do, Junk?'

'I don't know. I've not been doing anything for years.'

'Not even those anti-psychotic drugs you were prescribed at the hospital?'

'No. They were stolen,' Junk admitted.

'Fuck, no. Really? That's like stealing a cripple's wheelchair, isn't it? Stealing prescription medicines off a nut. That is low.'

Burgess paused, he was ready for his cocaine. His nose was edging towards the starting line, Bernard's tenner hovering below his nostril. Then he pulled himself back once more. It seemed he was going to make himself wait. Using the rolled note as a baton to make his point he began harassing Junk again.

'I asked about drugs killing you, because I'm not so sure. For instance, you're not dead. I'm not dead. That kid who died the other night wasn't killed by the amount of drugs he'd done. I'd say that people killed you. I'd say that Paul Sorel, in particular, is back here to kill me. What would you say?'

'I'd say that you're right,' said Junk.

'He's going to kill me because I raped him.'

'That's the story,' said Junk.

Burgess returned to the line. From way above him, Junk waited for the vacuuming suck, the throaty gasp. Burgess's face streaming with tears. But Burgess wasn't finished yet.

'Is that what you reckon? I raped Paul?' Burgess was flushed, either with indignation or with coke-lust. 'I tell you, that's a sack of fucking shit. Isn't that right, Bernie?'

Bernard shook his head. 'Yes, Chief.'

'There you are. Bernard says it's crap. What do you say?'

'I don't know. I'm just saying what I heard. Paul would come back for you and kill you, because of what you did to him.'

'Fuck that. Fucking gossip. I did nothing. When he escaped from Risley, who set that up? Do you think Michael Cross did it alone?'

Junk said nothing.

'It was me that set it up. I got him out of Risley. I paid Michael to do it, I set up the whole fucking deal. So, you see, it's shit. I did nothing except help Paul.' Burgess took another preparatory pass over the pile of the cocaine.

'But I tell you, if Paul does turn up now, then he's a fucking dead man-stroke-woman.'

Burgess went head down into the pile of powder. This was it. He swiped along the length of the line in one solid, five-second, inhalation. The burn at the back of his throat turned into an open-mouthed half-scream. There was no anaesthetising coolness to the powder, just the chemical aggression of speed. Burgess was staggering to his feet now. 'What the fuck?'

Bernard lifted up his pistol again and shot Junk.

TWENTY-EIGHT

A burst of machine-gun fire raked the planks around Bernard's feet, sending him rolling backwards to the edge of the dance floor. Giving him no time to celebrate his dead hit on Junk. He ended cowering beyond the wooden boards, taking cover beneath the eight-inch kerb that lifted the dance floor off the level of the club. As he went down, he saw Estela emerge from the cafeteria with her new machine pistol in her hand.

Burgess swung around, firing through his tears but blindly, racking and refiring without a hope. Estela ducked back behind the sheet of translucent rubber strips that hung like a curtain, screening off the Gravity's cafeteria. A lucky shot thudded against the sheeting but Estela's shadow continued walking along behind the curtain.

'Paul,' Burgess shouted. 'Is that you, Paul?'

'It's Estela, now. Hey, I love this club. It has a post-industrial feel. I find that sympathetic. Where did you get the curtains? Are they the kind that surround welding bays in factories? That's so cool, you know.'

Burgess had pulled himself up on to the stage and taken cover behind a stack of speakers. Estela heard him rack his gun again. He reappeared behind a bass bin to let off another shot. He was not even close. Estela stepped out between the rubber sheets and shot off a chunk of the speaker cabinet with her Heckler & Koch MP5K. It had a thirty-two round magazine and she had extra in her bag. She could keep this up all night.

'What do you think of this for a weapon, Burgess?' she shouted. 'I boosted it off a jackboy over in Moss Side.'

She drilled open the front of the stage before ducking back behind the curtains. Bernard lifted himself from the ground and took a couple of shots at her. One hit a pillar by the side of her head. Then, the few lights went out.

Junk must have managed to haul himself over to the lighting booth and pull the last of the switches. Only the light generated by the video show lit the club now. Estela had a choice. She could either attack from the front or return through the cellar bar, cut back through Burgess's office and climb the stairs behind the stage, close by the door that Junk had left opened for her. If she did that, she would emerge right behind Bernard and Burgess. That would surprise them.

Junk hit another button. Dry-ice began to fill the club. Estela opted for full-frontal exposure. She slipped out of the protective cover of the rubber sheeting and headed for the balcony stairs. If Bernard and Burgess continued shooting like that, they would only end up hitting each other. Burgess's sight might be clearing, but the way he shot – he could fire into a sauna without hitting flesh-tones. He was still flailing about the stage, wondering what kind of poison he had snorted. When Estela reached cover, behind a steel column, she had the time to tease him:

'How did you like the cocaine, Burgess?'

'It was speed, you fuck.' She heard him rack his shotgun; it was beginning to sound like a spastic nervous reflex.

'It was top quality speed, Burgess. You should know, you made it. Junk was just giving it back to you.'

Junk sent a carbine of lights spinning out over the field of dry-ice, raking the clouds below with flares of red, yellow, blue. Somewhere below Estela, a shotgun crackled.

'Who are you trying to hit, Burgess?'

His voice came up through the cushion of smoke: 'You, you cunt.'

'Why?' she asked. 'What did I do to you?'

He had stopped shooting now. He would be trying to work out where she was standing from the direction of her voice. He was still behind the speaker stack, Estela was sure. She circled the balcony and listened. Her high heels tapped against the steel mesh flooring. She could not pin-point Bernard. If he was below her, he could not get a clear shot.

'How is Bernard? He has such a little itty bit gun, I bet he's scared to death. Now that he's playing with the big girls.'

The dry-ice was beginning to clear and Bernard was no longer lying by the dance floor. She should be able to place him. He was so heavy, every step he made would be audible. The footsteps she could hear were too far away. From their sound, the time they kept as they walked in paired formation, it was the police.

Estela waited until the first blue cap appeared before strafing the stage. One policeman flung himself backwards and made the cover of the door. The other tripped and sprawled across the floor. Where he lay, he could only be a yard or so from Burgess. Estela wondered what Burgess would do. If he was behind the speakers, crouching, clutching his shotgun, the policeman must be staring straight into Burgess's speed-frazzled face.

Bursts of rapid static, the crackle of a police radio. The policeman who had made the stairwell was asking for assistance. His partner lay spread-eagled on the stage, lit in a solitary pool of light. Junk was playing with the spotlights, lighting the policeman like a theatrical corpse, although the man was certainly unhurt. Estela could see his bottom rise in the air as he tried to wiggle up-stage commando-style. She aimed the Heckler & Koch at the speaker stacks, one more time. As the cabinet splintered open, the magnetic coils and the speaker cones flew out in pieces.

The policeman stopped playing dead. Leaping to his feet, he charged for the door and made it. Estela still could not see Burgess; but as she had not seen him, he could not have moved. He must be shell-shocked, hidden behind the bass bin.

The policemen had made it to the street, probably praying, probably thanking whatever God, gods or spirits ruled their houses that they still had breath left to run. Bernard, large and heavy-footed, was the last unpredictable element. Estela came away from the balustrade. She pulled the magazine out of her gun and flung it aside, taking the fresh one from her bag.

She expected to find Junk half-way along the gantry, sat in the lighting box, playing with the disco lights and enjoying the show. She found him dusted with speed, sprinkled with fairy light glitter, with a bullet in his head.

Estela saw the wound only when she was already beside him. From the way he was sitting, by the marionette twitches of his hands on the lighting controls, she had already guessed that something was wrong. The Doctor Frankenstein pose – Oh Lord, What Have I Wrought? – waiting for the lightning to strike his home. His two glassy eyes were fixed outfront, rigid, almost on stalks. He was sat at the lighting controls, watching the entertainment unfold below through the glass front of the cabin. The bullet had entered his head around the bottom of his left ear. The exit wound spread from the back of the ear to the nape of the neck. He had lost a good quarter of the left hemisphere. Estela guessed that it was gone for good (who would go looking? Who would scoop it up?). She moved to his better side, whispered 'John, John' in his right ear, but he kept his eyes forward. If he was in pain, the only sign that she could see was the tight grimace on his lips. He could not speak – she was sure that he could not speak. Saliva had welled into a froggy amphetamine froth along the set line of his mouth.

Estela took Junk's hand and watched the scene below with him. The disco lights ran through changing patterns as Junk's finger continued to dance across the controls. The dry-ice had cleared. Over on the stage, Burgess's head appeared around a speaker cabinet. The shotgun followed, then the rest of him. He racked the gun, but let it lie in the crux of his left arm. He was fiddling in his pocket. When he brought out an envelope, Estela thought: What's this? His last will and testament? He burrowed his nose into the envelope and came up powdered in white dust. Estela watched as Burgess plunged back into the packet of speed, aching for a little sulphate courage.

It was clear that Burgess could not see Bernard, either. He was staring wild-eyed around the club, looking lost. The shotgun was back in his hands. He was prowling across the front of the stage like The Great White Hunter. If he had sense, he would run. There was nothing he could do while he stayed inside the club.

Estela stroked the back of Junk's hand. He had left the door off the latch for her. Had he also thought about her getaway? Behind a locked door in the cocktail bar was a flight of stairs. At the bottom she would find a firedoor. If Junk had opened the first door, she could kick open the firedoor and she was free.

The Gravity backed on to the canal. She was supposed to escape along the towpath. It was too late to ask Junk for further directions. She patted his hand, stood, and took another look at Burgess. He was a sitting target, walking along the stage like that, his nose fizzing at the edges.

Estela had never credited Bernard with the finesse to catch her from behind. He came on his tiptoes.

'I had a woman with plastic tits, once. They were all right. They didn't go so floppy when she was on her back, if you know what I mean.'

He had surprised her. Her gun lay flat to the lighting desk, too far away to be useful. She said, 'Hello, Bernard. What do we do now?'

Walking through the door, his shoulders all but touched both sides of the door jamb. He knew that he had her, he could afford to take his time.

'I guess old John Quay's not so much of a threat, is he? That's some fucking wound. You could put your fucking fist in there, if you're into fucking fisting.'

He poked at the wound with interest. The gun in his other hand was a Beretta, much like the one she should have been using. 'Nice piece,' she said.

'It's all right. Pretty accurate, I guess,' he said. 'I mean, I'm the only one who's got a fucking result tonight. I doubt if Burgess could hit the side of a freight train, the state he's in.'

He pushed the Beretta up against her cheek.

'We'd better be going, eh?' he said. 'Oh yeah, and if you could just hand over that huge fuck-off gun you've got there.'

She picked up the Heckler & Koch and passed it over, before turning to walk out of the room ahead him. He had the Beretta at her back. He stopped her at the door. He told her – turn around.

She was facing him. He pushed the Beretta under one tit while he felt at the other one.

'Not bad. If I just rip away some of this cloth . . . tasty bit of lingerie, that.'

He pulled the breast up over the top of the bra cup.

'Not much of a nipple, is it. They're never going to get rock, no matter how cold it gets. Nice aureole, though. Is that fake?'

'Yes, the skin is treated and coloured.'

'It looks natural. Did you finish the whole job, yet? Are you all woman?'

'Not completely.'

'You haven't still got a dick, have you? Oh, don't say that.'

Estela did not say anything. Bernard slipped his hand under the front of her dress, pushing his hand between her legs as he pushed her backwards. She staggered. She had to open her legs to keep her balance. Bernard's huge fat hand cradled the whole of her crotch.

'There's no dick, there. At least, I don't think there is.'

He felt around, carefully. 'I'm not sure what there is, though. Plenty of padding – how much underwear have you got on?'

'This is Manchester. It's not stopped raining since I arrived. I don' want to risk catching a chill.'

'It feels like you've got on one of those body-stockings, besides a pair of tights and your panties. It's a bit bulbous. I can't make out your crack. Is that it?'

He was grinding a finger into her groin. Hard enough to hurt. He was pushing at a spot that was never going to give.

'What is it?'

'I'm on the rag,' Estela told him. He looked up at her in surprise.

There was no time for him to ask more questions. Following a huge crash, the whole side of the building shook. Bernard was too startled to continue his abuse.

He pushed his Beretta even harder into her ribs and tried to look down through the window of the lighting booth. Estela felt the balcony shake, but could not see what was going on.

Bernard twisted her by the neck: 'Get down those fucking stairs.'

TWENTY-NINE

Amjad faced down the street. The Gravity stood to his right, looming over the canal-side in a Mancunian sulk. He knew he should get going. When he dropped Estela off, she had never said to wait. He knew that if he were going to hang around, he'd spend the night in police custody. He'd seen two cops enter, already. He watched as they slid through the side door, looking pleased with themselves. Five minutes later, they'd come out full tilt, running fit to burst. The sound of gunfire hung in the air long after they disappeared. Any second, a whole police battalion would surround the club. He should go while he still could. But he stayed, transfixed by the set of powerful headlights that came swinging towards him.

The brewery truck had appeared from Deansgate, careering under the weight of a tankerful of Boddingtons. It was definitely hijacked. It was driven by a madman, going miles too fast. The truck jack-knifed in the middle of the road, the tanker rolling dangerously behind the cab.

There was a steel-shuttered roll-door, almost two storeys high, built into the side of the club. Amjad watched as the truck rammed against it, the steel slats buckling at the first assault. The truck jolted backwards, rearing up on its giant tyres. In that second, Amjad recognised Michael Cross. He was the driver. Sat around him, nothing but a set of motherfucker gangsters. The Taz-Man and his crew, armed to the fucking teeth.

The wagon was thrown into reverse four, perhaps five, times – taking that many head-on collisions before it tore through the steel doors. To Amjad, only yards away in his Nissan, the sound and the din were deafening. The demolition of the steel shutters and the tearing of metal on metal were followed by automatic fire. The brewery truck trashed, smashed to fuck and shot to pieces.

Bernard kicked at her behind. Estela stumbled down the steps in her heels, still trying to re-dress, to fold her titties back inside her body-stocking. Another two crashes, and the whole of the Gravity shook. It could not be a bomb. It must be a juggernaut.

Bernard's hand in the small of her back sent her sprawling towards the dance floor. She slid face down across the wooden boards, picking up traces of broken glass that littered the floor and snagged her flesh. She kept her handbag tight.

As she fell, she saw Burgess stumbling over towards the roll-door, aiming his shotgun. Bernard faced the doors head on, holding her Heckler & Koch. As the doors gave way, a diesel truck pounded through. Even from the floor, Estela could see that Michael Cross was driving. Beside him sat the Taz-Man, his jackboys riding shotgun inside the cab. She couldn't see what kind of arms they carried. She had a Tech–9 in her bag, so Michael had better keep his head low. Everyone began firing as the truck roared towards her. She was still drawing her gun when Bernard went up, blown into confetti under a solid wall of gunfire. She ran.

The flashing blue lights were behind him, dancing in his rearview mirror. The sirens filled the air. The police were coming from all directions. Where the hulk of the truck stuck out from the twisted steel shutters, Amjad saw a figure trying to squeeze out. He watched as the man ducked beneath the undercarriage of the beer tanker. He started his car, moving slowly towards the running man but ready to speed off. As he recognised Michael Cross, he reached behind his seat to throw open the back door. He shouted: 'Crossy, Crossy, get the fuck in here, man.'

Michael Cross came across the road, tilting forward as he sprinted. He leapt, dived head-first into the car and Amjad rammed the pedal down to the Nissan's floor. The blue lights filled the rearview mirror. If any one car was sent to chase him, he would lose the fucker, for sure. They would not have a licence number; all they could have seen were one more anonymous Nissan and its Paki driver. They could trail over Manchester from now until the end of the world, they wouldn't catch him, he told himself. He hoped.

Michael Cross had managed to turn himself around and slammed the passenger door shut. He had his eyes forward, to where another stream of police cars and wagons had appeared. The whole area swarmed with blue lights. Amjad tried to force down the rate of his breathing; keep it steady, keep it steady. His car passed alongside the police convoy. He held the Nissan to forty miles an hour, the police shot past without looking. He was safe, which he just could not fucking believe.

'Amjad? It's Amjad isn't it?'

'Yeah, Crossy. What the fuck was that?'

'Hell. Hell-fucking-hell. Just this deafening, deafening ... fucking bullets ... I don't know, a fucking war.' Michael Cross was shaking, he didn't even know how much.

'What were you doing?'

'Driving. I was driving the fuckers. One second, I was chilling in a club. Next, the Taz-Man's holding a gun to my head and I'm hijacking a fucking wagon. Shit. Shit Shit. How many police?'

Another convoy flooded the dual carriageway with dancing blue light and sirens. Princess Road seemed to disintegrate under the force of the noise.

'How many? I don't fucking know, Crossy.' Amjad felt himself collapsing under the pressure to take it slowly, choking on his own adrenalin.

'What happened in the club?'

'It's destroyed.'

'Is anyone dead?'

'Yeah, obviously, totally. As we smashed through the doors, Bernard was right in front of us. I saw him lifted into the air, knocked back about twenty feet, shot to pieces.'

'What about Estela?'

'I don't know if she's injured or dead, or what. Once we were through the doors. I just wanted to get out. The noise, the smoke, some lunatic was playing with the disco lights – it was fucking madness. I tell you, I was scared to fucking death.'

'What about Burgess, then?'

'Don't know. But the place is trashed. He's finished, if he's still alive.'

Amjad said, 'Someone else should run that place. What I thought, I should tell my cousin about it.'

'I could live with that. That would be a happy ending.'

THIRTY

Synapses splice this scene. Fuck this shutter down, steel bases. The Junkmeister at the controls, in the house, in the place to be. Shredding these walls like they weren't copacetic, crushing this hall without the aid of anaesthetic. Let the hells of hipperty ring, freedom got an AK. On the wing, on the scream, the windscreen blown out – is that friendly-fire? Reread those positions, grandmaster. The Junkster spies artillery on the downward flank, he greets the dervs with a barrage of halogen strobe and frosts the suckers. We have the technology to trace all elements with laser-accuracy, set the pin-spot to the mirror-ball and let the wheel of destiny dispose of each man according to his lights. The doors are open, come out blazing my jollies.

We have no control over the following inserts. Truss meek ill me, the Junker knows what he sees. A container-truck of crack black firepower. Burned, bouncing and burning, faces them down. Perforated, he bites the wax. Blat Blat Blat. Line up the Blues with the Green and hit the canisters. Dry-ice this shot-down scene. The Junkster's feeling jake.

THIRTY-ONE

Estela rested a compact mirror against the sauce bottle and arranged her new wig. 'This was a beautiful choice, Theresa. I always felt that I could be a blonde trapped in the body of a brunette.'

Theresa was impatient. 'Tell me what happened.'

'As the police stormed through the side doors, Junk filled the club with dry-ice. There was nothing to see, but everyone carried on shooting. I slipped away.'

'Was that planned?'

'I don' know, darling,' Estela admitted that she had lost track of the plan some time ago.

According to the tickets that Theresa had bought her, the train would leave in half an hour. It was cold in the station café but for the first time since she had arrived, the rain had stopped. Shafts of heavenly light pierced the clouds, selecting ornamental details on the façade of the Corn Exchange. Estela stopped tugging at the fringe of her new blonde wig and admired her last view.

Theresa said, 'You never had any intention of killing Burgess, had you?'

The morning edition of the *Evening News* was spread out on the table between them. Beside the main story, an account of the siege at the Gravity between a drugs gang and the police, there was a boxed item on Burgess. The paper gave an account of his life story, speculated on his past drug links, and reported his arrest the previous night on drug and firearm charges. The photograph showed him in handcuffs as he was led away by DI Green. DI Green wore a flak jacket over a navy suit.

'He raped you. Didn't you want to kill him for that?'

'He never tried to rape me. He said that he loved me. He paid Michael to break me out of prison. But what could I do? I was never attracted to him. He would beg me and beg me. On the night I escaped from the remand centre, Michael drove me to meet him. We found Burgess prowling around the offices of a broken-down club in Longsight, out of his mind on speed and vodka. He asked Michael to wait in the bar, saying that he needed to speak to me privately.

'The second we were alone, he fell to his knees in front of me and held up his hands, as if he was praying. I remember he had tears in his eyes. He pleaded with me to let him suck me off. He told me that he would give me anything. I could have thousands, if he could have my cock in his mouth.'

'Did you let him?'

'No. I tried to push him to one side, but only gently. I didn't want to hurt his feelings. He started shouting and shouting. Michael Cross came running back into the room. He saw Burgess on his knees, pulling at the buttons on the fly of my jeans. I was still wearing prison uniform, a brown denim jacket and matching trousers. Burgess was in a fury now and almost screaming. I looked over at Michael, the shock on his face. I kicked Burgess over, then just stepped over him and walked away. Burgess lay on the floor screaming that he would kill me.

'I made Michael drive me around to Burgess's house. I knew it was over and I needed money, so I cleared out his safe. I took the money he had promised me. Then I took off for Brazil. That was fifteen years ago, and everyone believed that he had tried to rape me and that I had robbed him.'

Theresa had one more question.

'Yen saw those photographs of Burgess, in an envelope alongside the gun. You were arranging a hit on Burgess. That's why you were here, isn't it? Burgess was a money launderer and people wanted him dead.'

'He was a money launderer, yes. All those bits of computer papers you gave me, I left them in Burgess's office, along with a kilo of cocaine I stole off the Taz-Man. Once the police find all of that, then they will go through Burgess's accounts and work out his links to the international cocaine game.

'I was meant to have him killed, but there's no need. He'll go to prison, and I'll leave him alone – no matter how attractive it sounds in fiction, I never liked men's prisons.'

There was also a red wig. Theresa had brought a selection. It might have come down to a choice between the fiery red or the sulky blonde. Both could look dramatic – either a demon or an angel. But Estela knew where her heart lay. She wanted a wig to replace the one the police confiscated, the Debbie Harry wig she was wearing on the night she was arrested. A pouting angel in punky drag. Certainly, an angel . . .

'I saved Burgess's life,' she said. It was one way of looking at it. 'It's true, I never wanted to kill Burgess. Why should I? Everyone hated Burgess because he's a lunatic. But they are all so nostalgic for the old days, the time when Burgess was the Speed King and they worked for him. I never hated Burgess and I didn' want to kill him. After all, he did say he loved me.'

'Junk wasn't nostalgic for the old days. The drugs almost destroyed him. Then, we end up saving Burgess while Junk dies.'

Theresa had not got any of it right. Junk was not destroyed by the drugs, they had made him. Like a chemical version of destiny, drugs can make you into the kind of person you need to be. Junk was more than nostalgic, he was absorbed by the past. More than absorbed, he was suspended in the past like crystals dissolved in water. And according to the *Manchester Evening News*, he was not yet quite dead. So, there was still hope for him.